MURDER ON VOODOO ISLAND

A MYSTERY

J. KENT HOLLOWAY

Murder on Voodoo Island (A Kaitlyn Faust Mystery)

Previously publishing as Kaitlyn Faust

Copyright © 2022 by J. Kent Holloway

Published by Charade Media, LLC

Murder on Voodoo island (A Captain Joe Mystery)

Previously published as Killypso Island

Paperback ISBN: 979-8-9876847-0-2

Copyright © 2023 by J. Kent Holloway

Published by Charade Media, LLC

PROLOGUE

Island of St. Noel
Lesser Antilles
The Caribbean
February 10, 1955

I t's funny when you consider how quickly the place you call 'home' can turn from paradise to a hell on Earth. It can happen in the blink of an eye. Or in the amount of time it takes for someone to slip a mickey in my cup of joe. If anyone knows, it's me.

Right now, as a matter of fact. Although I'm not quite sure why yet. My brain's still fuzzy. I'm lying face down on a hardwood floor. That much, I'm aware of. But I haven't opened my one eye yet. I'm afraid if I do, it'll pop straight out of my head. That's how much my head's pounding right now.

My ears are working fine, though.

There's a commotion all around me. Shouts. Angry, nasty shouts. Boots shuffle along the floor around me. There's a struggle—more yelling, and the sound of fists hitting flesh and clothes ripping. It's somewhere behind me, but I'm not sure how far away. All I know is that people are angry. And the inside of my head feels as though a million bees are swarming around my gray matter—stinging every inch of it as they pass.

I groan. I can hear that, too. Feel the dryness of my throat, like sandpaper rubbing along even sandier paper.

Oh, I need a drink.

Then again, there's a sneaky part of me that says that's how I got into this mess to begin with. Rum.

More boots scurry past me, but I don't have strength enough to lift my head to see who it is.

No, it wasn't rum. It was the coffee. It had to be. It was that molten hot caffeine-laden cup of coffee that did this to me. I'm sure of it. So, where does that put me? Home? Eubank, Kentucky? If I could, I'd shake my head at the thought. I haven't been back there since before the war. Only other person I know who can make apple pie moonshine the way my mom could is...

My eye snaps open, but I still don't move.

"Chief, he's waking up." The voice sounds familiar, but I can't quite place it.

"I'll kill 'im!" Another familiar voice says. A voice I've called friend for several years now. So, why can't I place it? "I'll kill 'im for what he's done!"

The voice is angry. Mad with grief. And although I'm not sure why, I know that anger is directed squarely at me.

I groan again and try desperately to place my hands against the wooden floorboards to lift myself up. But I can't, for two reasons. First, my arms feel like rubber. There's no strength in them at all. But that's not the bad part. The second reason is the bad part. I can't place my hands against the floor because they're behind my back and can't move.

Tied?

No. I hear metal against metal as I shift my arms. Some-

2

one's put me in irons. Shackles or handcuffs, I'm not sure. I try to turn my head, but now all I can see with my burning eye is a pair of shoe soles moving to and fro around the small room.

The room.

What room am I in?

I can feel a nice gust of cool air washing down over me, along with the gentle *thump-thump-thump* of an overhead ceiling fan. My one good eye searches for more clues. Wood paneled walls are all around me, covered here and there with red velvet curtains pulled back with gold-tasseled ties. A bookshelf filled with a healthy selection of leather bound books is to my right.

The room is starting to take shape and, like the angry voice, it's familiar. I've been here before. Lots of times. Lots of pleasant memories are hazily edging their way in from the back of my mind.

Though I can't see it properly from my position on the floor, I know with certainty that there's a round wooden table a few feet away. A table with a bowl filled with water and tea leaves resting next to an ornate crystal ball.

The ball is purely decorative. The tea leaves aren't.

"Get him off da floor," an authoritative voice says. That one, I recognize immediately. Chief Fidel Armad, the commanding officer of the St. Noel Police Force.

What's he doing here?

Before I can ponder the question properly, two sets of beefy hands take hold of me by the armpits and haul me to my feet. They're not gentle about it either.

"Take him to the station for questioning," Armad continues. "And contact Martinique when you get there. The Inspector will want to hear about the murder."

Murder? What murder?

My head still feels as though the New York Philharmonic is

playing Beethoven's Fifth inside my skull. My eye struggles to focus. I look down at my feet. My Colt .45 is lying casually on the floor, as if it's been there since the day it was first produced.

I don't remember pulling my gun. Though I'm still struggling to piece together where I am, I know that in this room, I'd never need to use it. Not here. Never here.

But I can now smell the distinctly acrid scent of gun smoke hanging in the air. It's unmistakable. So I must have fired it.

Right?

"I swear to all da loa, you will suffer for what you did to 'er, Joe!" The same angry, but familiar, voice is shouting at me in that typical singsong lilt of the islands. "Da loa will give me my revenge! I swear to you!"

What did I do? And to whom?

I wish my head would stop throbbing. Wish I could focus. Maybe I could explain myself, if I could only think straight.

The police officers behind me begin to whirl me around to the parlor's open French doors. As I turn, I see her.

Angelique Lagrange.

My knees buckle at the sight. If the officers weren't gorilla-sized lugs disguised in sharp uniforms, I would have dropped to the floor. Angelique Lagrange, the Candyman's wife, lies on her back on the other side of her fortune-teller table. A gruesome red hole has been carved into her skull, just above the wide, staring eyes. Blood pools underneath her caramel-hued, voluminous body, staining her pretty floral-print dress with its crimson ugliness.

Oh, God. Angelique.

I turn my head toward the doors. Darkened paper lanterns hang sadly from lamp posts throughout town. The streets are covered in multi-colored confetti, empty rum bottles, and vomit—all telltale signs of the festivities the night before. The sky is overcast and gray, but the heat of the morning smacks me across the face in an instant splash of perspiration.

My eye surveys the street just outside the French doors, and my heart skips a beat. Behind the sawhorse barricade and amid the crowd of wide-eyed gawkers, stands Jacque 'the Candyman' Lagrange in all his immense glory. The man I've called 'friend' for nearly a decade. Now, he has murder in his fiery eyes, and it's directed entirely at me.

The officers escort me through the doors and into the teeming street. Shouts and howls fill the early morning air. The islanders are just as angry as Jacques. People I've called friends for the last decade are all looking at me like I'm the devil incarnate. In their eyes, I've betrayed them all. Killed their *mamba*— voodoo priestess—and the wife of the high priest. There's no greater insult. Especially from someone they've welcomed with open arms.

I try to speak. To offer an apology…an explanation. But my mouth is numb. I don't know if it's from the drug that knocked my lights out or from the shock of seeing poor Angelique as cold and as unmoving as a tombstone.

The officers push me through the street, and they're not too keen on keeping me out of the reach of the angry crowd. Hands grasp for me, tearing at my hair and my clothes. I swivel away, only to draw closer to other hands, equally as eager to slice off a piece of me.

My eye wanders the crowd. A few sad, concerned faces pop out among the throng. Good old Nessie—the unofficial matriarch of the island—stands off to my left, her head bowed in silent prayer, except for the brief moment she looks up and offers a brief nod of encouragement in my direction. Trixie Faye is standing next to her, her arm resting comfortingly over Nessie's shoulder. Trixie's blonde curls are radiant in the morning light, like the halo on an angel. Her brow is creased with worry, and she refuses to look me in the eye.

Not that she has much time to do so. The coppers jostle me forward, until we reach the waiting police car. They shove me in the backseat and begin driving toward the police station. It's not the first time I've been a guest there, but it's certainly going to be the first time I've been there under suspicion of murder. The murder of a dear friend at that.

What happened last night? Why can't I remember?

As the car barrels down the dust-filled road toward the station, my eye catches another set of faces. Three well-dressed men in black suits stand toward the back of the crowd, watching the drama with great interest. As we drive past, they each look at me through the backseat window. Two of them have nice purple shiners under their eyes. Another has a busted lip and a bandaged head under his fedora. Curious grins stretch across each of their faces. I have memories of those faces, too. And they're not fond ones.

I lean back in my seat, close my eye, and focus on remembering everything.

CHAPTER 1

Thirty-eight hours earlier

B efore we get started, first thing you should know is that the name's Joe Thacker. 'Captain Joe' to the locals of St. Noel, the Caribbean paradise I've called home for the last ten years—ever since the War. To a thirty-five-year-old, retired Navy pilot , born and raised in the landlocked hills of eastern Kentucky, St. Noel is probably as close to heaven as anyone could get with his feet set firmly on ground or ship's deck.

With only two seasons—warm and breezy—the island is almost always paradise. The jungle's lush and vibrant with life. The beaches are white sand and crystal blue water capped in white foam, with scantily clad natives frolicking in the waves. The islands have flowers with colors I've never learned the names of, and there's seafood that'll make your mouth water just from the smell coming from the grill.

And then, there're the people. God, how I love the people here. Being from the southern United States, I was raised with a certain set of values. Hospitality was up toward the top of that list, and the citizens of St. Noel, despite their meager means and being under the thumb of the French government by means of a greedy governor, are nothing if not hospitable to most outsiders that come to their island refuge.

So, when I pull *The Ulysses Dream*, my forty-two-foot Wheeler Cruiser, into Port Lucine and tether her to my slip, I'm not at all surprised to be greeted by the beaming smiles and waving hands of almost twelve children running up the dock.

"Captain Joe!" they shout as they run. Their chocolate and caramel-hued bodies glisten with perspiration from working all day in the sugar cane fields, but their energy as they approach seems to know no limits. "Captain Joe! *Ou se tounen!*"

Others in the group repeat in English, knowing I haven't become fluent in their Creole language just yet. "You're back!"

I laugh, moving aft and hefting four large wooden crates I've been hauling onto a dolly cart. Then I wheel them down the gangplank onto the dock before waving back at the kids.

"Bonjou, timoun yo!" Rough translation? 'Hello, kids.' It's one of the few Creole phrases I know.

I give them a wave after adjusting my eyepatch, to ensure the scarred, gaping cavity that once housed my eye isn't showing. The kids are fascinated by the injury, but I'm in no mood to regale them with stories about how I lost it for the thousandth time. Besides, I can never remember which story I've told them. And quite frankly, I have too much work to do to get sidetracked by tall tales.

Checking to ensure I've unloaded all the cargo I brought back from Havana, I move back onto the boat, slip my Colt .45 in my shoulder holster, and withdraw the boat's key from the dashboard. Then I give a short whistle with my thumb and forefinger pressed against my lips. A moment later, a tiny, black, fur-covered face pops up from the cabin belowdecks.

"Come on, Moe," I say to the three-year-old vervet monkey that adopted me against my will a few years earlier, when I was visiting Mozambique. "We've got work to do."

The monkey scowls at me before glancing back down to the cabin.

"No, you can sober up out here just as easily." The kids' excited shouts amplify when they realize the monkey is above deck. Ignoring the children, Moe hurls a sling of screeches at me. "Oh, no. You shouldn't have snuck into the whiskey, you banana head."

He shrieks at me again.

"Don't take that tone with me. You're not staying, and that's final. I don't trust you to be drunk by yourself, after that little fiasco on St. Thomas."

Moe lets out a disappointed raspberry, then scampers across the deck, up my leg, and finally onto my shoulder. He wraps his tail around my neck, then glances down at the kids on the dock before leaping down into their midst for a barrage of belly rubs and ear scratches.

"Hey, don't encourage him," I say, as I climb onto the dock. "That flea bag's hard enough to deal with, without you guys spoiling him like that."

I watch in secret delight as they continue playing with the monkey, giving me time to light up a cigar and enjoy the smooth tobacco as it wafts down my throat. A moment later, I notice a sudden hush along the dock. I look down to see all the children staring at the crates with wide, eager eyes.

"Oh, no. Uh-uh," I say, shaking my head. "Don't even think about it."

They look from the crates to me, then back again. A few of their little bare legs begin to bounce up and down excitedly, their smiles stretching to impossible lengths as the sudden realization of my cargo begins to manifest in their greedy little heads. The boys, all wearing cutoff shorts and no shirts or shoes, are covered head-to-foot in grime, dirt, and flecks of sugar cane. One of the boys, Malik, stands there with his baseball mitt on one hand and an old wooden bat I gave him for Christmas in the other. The girls, ever so demure with their hands behind their backs and offering coy smiles as they look up at me with saucer-sized eyes, are dressed in pretty flower-print dresses they received from missionaries last year. The dresses are already stretching uncomfortably over their growing, but emaciated frames.

"I said no... I can't..."

They turn their pleading eyes to me again before the entire dock explodes in a round of excited shouts of joy. Around twenty-four hands instantly shoot up toward me, tenaciously begging for a taste of what I've just hauled back from Cuba.

I take another puff from the cigar and give them a sly wink with another shake of my head.

"You know I can't give you any," I say, grabbing the dolly from the deck of my boat and sliding it under the crate nearest me. Moe, curious as to why the children have suddenly abandoned him, jumps up onto the crate and takes several sniffs. His own eyes swell to nearly twice their size as he smells the confectionary treats inside. "Candyman's voodoo will turn me into a toad, or a goat, or something, if I hand out his stash to the lot of you."

The children moan, their excited faces melting into masks of disappointment. I stare at them disapprovingly for a second or two, wanting to savor the moment for as long as I can. Of course, this is a game we always play whenever I get back from a run, and they play their parts to the nines.

After another few moments of delectable torture, I allow

myself a grin, still clutching the cigar between my teeth. I dig into the pockets of my leather flight jacket, and pull out heaps of foiled candy in the palms of my hands.

Their faces light up when they see the colorful bounty, and their feet begin stomping the deck in anticipation as I begin passing out pieces of chocolate, hard candies, and licorice sticks to each of them. With nods of genuine thanks, they dig into the candy, just as the island's chief customs agent and a porter make their way up to my boat.

"Cap'n Joe, you spoil d'ose childr'n too much," the customs agent says, as he extends his hand. I accept it and give it a firm shake in return. I keep my eye trained on both men as best I can, while feeling reassured by the gun hanging from its shoulder holster on my left side.

I can't believe they're here. After the last haul, I thought we'd come to an arrangement.

"That's funny, Monday. I was just sayin' the same thing to them about the monkey."

Monday Renot, Port Lucine's chief customs agent, is a bear of a man, standing a little over six feet tall and weighing an easy two hundred and fifty pounds. He's darker skinned than most on the island, who typically have mixed blood to some extent or another. He also has a reputation for being a mean drunk and a nasty brawler, when he isn't flitting his usually ill-gotten money away in the local gambling dens. Even worse, as the chief customs agent, he's one of the many corrupt public servants working for the despot governor the French government sent. And I trust him about as much as I could pick him up and throw him.

That being said, he isn't all bad. We've shared a few games of poker over the years and have always gotten along decently enough. His greed and his general laziness have been major boons for my business on more than one occasion. That is, until the Governor's and the Candyman's lifelong feud flared to life again a few months ago. Since then, Monday's been a thorn in my side at every turn—even confiscating my cargo completely, on my last trip.

The pleasantries over, Monday eyes the four crates. One of his eyebrows lift unnaturally high over his eye. "You realize I need to check what's inside, right, *mon ami*?"

"Ah, come on, Monday. Not again." I shrug. "I thought we had a deal."

The dock is suddenly quiet. I look down and notice all the kids have spirited themselves away, leaving nothing but wrappers to tumble along the boards with the wind. Moe, resting his haunches on one of the crates, is watching our exchange with great interest.

Monday sniffs, hiking up his britches over his rotund belly. His brow crinkles.

"Ah, geez, don't be this way, Monday."

"You and I both know d'at Governor Lagrange is bucklin' down on smugglin' on d'is island, Joe."

"But this ain't about smuggling, and you know it. It's about the Governor's grudge against the Candyman—his own brother." I spread my arms in a gesture of peace. "Why on Earth would you let the petty squabbles of powerful men like those ruin a perfectly lovely relationship between the two of us?"

This is pettiness to the extreme. Governor Lagrange has his hands in just about every illegal enterprise on the island, from drugs to gambling to prostitution. His brother, the Candyman, has only cut out a small little niche among the island's vices: liquor, which the Governor has taxed almost to non-existence for legitimate tavern owners on the island.

Everyone knows there are only two things I smuggle… guns and booze. Monday knows exactly what I've shipped in from Cuba for the Candyman. This is nothing more than a shake down. A raising of hackles. Whose balls are bigger? And it's starting to irk me to no end.

The large man grunts. "Governor Lagrange is my employer, *mon ami*. He puts food on da table for my family…"

"So have I, if you'll recall…"

Monday gives me an apologetic nod, but he won't let me finish. "…and he's given us strict instructions to make life miserable for da *Candymon* more d'an anyone else on St. Noel." The customs agent pauses, then looks around conspiratorially. "But between you and me, he's gotten much worse ever since d'ose white men in suits showed up."

I perk up at that. "Men in suits? The French?"

Monday shakes his head.

"Then, who are they?"

"Nobody knows. D'ey showed up t'ree days ago while you were in Cuba. Flew into port on an island jumper from Trinidad. They went straight to da Governor's villa. Been stayin' at Nessie's free of charge ever since."

That isn't good news. St. Noel is small enough to avoid the casual tourism of most Caribbean islands. It isn't that St. Noel couldn't use the tourist business, or that it wouldn't be one heck of a tourist destination. It's just that the people here really enjoy their way of life, and tourism is discouraged because of it.

But strange men in suits—especially those in business with our governor—could only mean trouble for the people around here. For now, though, I don't have time to worry about it. The Candyman's festival is tomorrow evening at sundown, and I have a slew of things to do and people to see before then.

I need to take care of this customs inspection fast.

"Come on, Monday," I say, giving him my biggest smile while pulling out a wad of American cash from my pocket and flipping through the bills. "For old time's sake? Can't you just let this go, just this once? Think about the *Festivale de la Mort* tomorrow."

Monday looks from the money to the crates, scratching his patchy beard in thought. He opens his mouth to reply, just as the sound of children shouting echoes toward us from the other end of the pier. We turn to the sound, to see the kids that were here only a few minutes earlier are now running at full speed back in our direction. Behind them, waddling down the wooden planks, is the immense figure of Jacques 'the Candyman' Lagrange, and two of his beefy voodoo followers. I've never learned their names. Instead, I've just always called them 'King' and 'Kong.'

"Ooooh, buddy," I say, stuffing the cash back into my khakis and releasing a faux hiss of concern. "Should've been quicker on the take."

All the newcomers are dressed in the white linen trousers and shirts of the region, although the Candyman is sporting his customary wide-brimmed straw hat, which shades his massive bald head and the fat rolls down the back of his neck. Lagrange is almost double the girth of Monday, though most of his fat acts to hide the thick ropes of muscle underneath, which could easily crush a man's head with a squeeze of his thumb and forefinger. He's scowling as he approaches the customs agent and the porter, and I can sense that the two men are now frozen with fear.

I feel bad for them both. Kind of. But not really. Monday knows the deal. He's been around long enough to know you don't nickel-and-dime the Candyman, even if he is feeling pressure coming down from the governor's villa. Besides that, the mook has been a general pain in my side for years.

The children beam from ear to ear as they continue to chew and suck on the candy I've brought them. They playfully encircle us while providing space for the Candyman to enter our ranks. King and Kong stand back, their powerful arms crossed over equally powerful chests.

Ignoring Monday and the porter, the fat man looks at me for a moment, then smiles with a slight nod of his head. "Cap'n. You had a pleasant trip, I presume?"

I return the nod. The Candyman doesn't intimidate me like many others on the island. I know his secret. Though he's physically large, with a slag of a face, he's basically a quick-witted chap with a deep love for children and a contagious laugh when they're around. He's basically the voodoo version of Father Christmas, if you really want to know the truth. He's also not the one really in charge of his illegal operations. That privilege belongs to his wife, Angelique. Besides, he and I go farther back than anyone on this island. We're friends...of sorts...through common enterprises.

"It was pretty uneventful." I nod over at Monday with a roll of my eye. "Until now."

"So da childr'n 'ave told me." The fat man removes his hat, wiping a stream of sweat from his brow, before replacing it once more on his hairless head. He then looks over at Monday while stroking the bone and feather necklace around his meaty neck. "Mr. Renot, is d'ere a problem wit' my merchandise I should know about?"

Monday begins stammering, looking back and forth between me and the Candyman. His eyes are watering. I can almost hear his drying tongue begin to scrape against the roof of his mouth, as he tries to come up with some excuse for interfering in the voodoo priest's business.

"Monsieur Lagrange..." No one but his dearest friends are allowed to call him 'Candyman.' At least, to his face. "I... It's your brother... I mean..."

The Candyman's scowl deepens. He looks down at the kids, gives them a wink, then nods in the direction of the shore. Without comment, they scamper away from the scene, knowing full well how unwise it is to argue with the man when it comes to his business. As if sensing the coming danger, Moe leaps from the crate to my neck. He huddles close, with his eyes fixed on the action. I scratch him behind the ears and wait to see how this is going to play out.

"Lamont Kingston."

Ah, so that's the porter's last name... For the life of me, I couldn't remember it. The skinny dock worker steps toward the Candyman, his eyes downcast. He won't look at the immense man, mainly because of his beliefs.

"Open one of d'em crates," the Candyman says, raising an eyebrow at me in a silent question. I nod back at him with a smile. When Lamont doesn't move, the Candyman gestures toward the crate. "Go on, now. I give you my permission. I know you're just doin' what yer told, and you mean no malice toward me."

I'm not entirely sure of that. I've seen the weasel pocket his share of plenty of payoffs that I've made to Monday in the past. But I say nothing.

Lamont seems to go limp momentarily, then he exhales in relief as he walks over to the first crate and uses the crowbar he's been white-knuckling since the Candyman's arrival. He pries the nails up from the lid. A minute later, the lid pops off and everyone goes silent.

"Go ahead, Mr. Kingston," the Candyman urges. "Take a look inside."

Warily, the porter glances at his boss, then pulls out the heaps of straw filler inside the crate, until the contents are revealed for all to see. Bags upon bags pack the space, filled with every kind of candy imaginable to man. Four glass jars containing peppermint sticks, gumdrops, hard fruit-flavored candies, and an assortment of many others—all wrapped in shiny wrappers—seem to illuminate the inside of the crate like a cask of pirate gold. Monday, incredulous, steps forward and fumbles through the treasure with a dumb stare plastered on his face.

"I don't understand," he mutters, flipping over the candy containers one by one.

"Would you like to check da others as well, Mr. Renot?" the Candyman asks, a playful smile spreading across his voluminous face.

Monday steps away, shaking his head. "No, no. I've seen enough." He throws me a murderous glare. He knows what's happening here. It's the oldest smuggling trick in the book—hide the real stash in a false bottom of the crate. But the customs man is smart enough not to look a gift horse in the mouth. The Candyman is giving him a way out, and Monday's smart enough to take it.

"My apologies, Mr. Lagrange," Monday says, offering a slight bow of the head. "I am very sorry to inconvenience you, but you know... I must do my duty and ensure contraband doesn't find its way onto our beautiful island. Your brother wouldn't like that. You understand."

The Candyman laughs at that and slaps the customs agent on the shoulder playfully. "D'at's because my little brother lacks imagination and vision, Mr. Renot." He slaps Monday's shoulders again for good measure. "And he doesn't appreciate loyalty in his employees." He narrows his eyes at Monday. "Unlike me. D'at is, if you're ever looking for a new, more prosperous job."

"That will be quite enough of that," a voice calls out behind us.

We turn to see the tall skeletal form of Governor Lagrange, dressed in his crisply pressed military uniform and cap, marching down the pier's planks with the island's only three police officers right behind him. The officers are all armed with rifles, which are now resting on their right shoulders. They approach boldly, eyeing each of us with contempt, before stopping only a foot or so away from the Candyman.

"By decree of my office, dear brother," the Governor says. His voice is as smooth as Tennessee molasses; it's the exact opposite of the Candyman's booming gravelly one. "I've ordered Mr. Renot to confiscate the cargo brought here by this…" He sneers at me, then waves in my general direction with limp-wristed disinterest. "…person."

The Governor glances back at the officers, which includes Chief Fidel Armad, a man who probably despises me—and all white folk, really—more than anyone else on the island. "See to it that Mr. Renot and his porter are unmolested as they transport these crates back to the Customs Office."

The Chief, giving me a murderous smile, nods. The three coppers then remove their rifles from their shoulders, and take aim at each of us. The porter, Lamont Kingston, gulps and waits for instructions from his boss. Monday, obviously just as nervous, nods and waves the young man along. The crates are then lifted on top of one another on the dolly cart and wheeled away from us with a full police escort.

The Governor, who is looking his brother up and down with an upturned nose, chuckles as they leave.

"D'at wasn't necessary, Anton," the Candyman says. His voice comes out like a grizzly's growl. "We could 'ave worked somet'ing out, if you 'ad just talked wit' me."

"Our days of talking are over, dear brother. I'm officially placing you and your little bootlegging operation on notice." The Governor glances at me with a sniff. "As well as your own particular side business, American."

With that said, the scarecrow of a man turns and stomps off the pier, leaving me with the Candyman and his two disciples.

"Well, that could have gone better," I say, lifting my captain's cap and giving my scalp a scratch. Moe is trembling against my neck, obviously detecting the tension in the air.

The Candyman sniffs, but says nothing. He turns to his men and waves them ahead of us, as we stroll toward the island's only town, Port Lucine.

CHAPTER 2

" Before I forget, are you plannin' to come to da festival
tomorrow night?" Candyman asks, as if the ordeal
with his brother and our cargo hasn't just happened.
We're strolling down the dusty thoroughfare toward town. It's
easily a mile walk, and I'm rather surprised the fat man didn't
drive his Bentley to the dock when he came to confront
Monday. "Angelique says she's been missin' you. You 'aven't
come to see her in months."

I decide to take my cue from the voodoo priest and forget
everything, too. It's better to just take our lumps and enjoy the
late afternoon stroll. I take a pull from my cigar and exhale
away from him, as I gaze up at the purple-orange horizon
above the mango trees. The sun will be setting in the next hour
or so, and the temperature is already dropping to a comfortable
seventy-odd degrees. "Yeah, tell her I'm sorry about that. I've
been meaning to come by... You know how much I love her..."

"Her apple pie moonshine?" He chuckles. His laugh is so
deep, I can almost feel it vibrating through me. "Just like yer
mom used to make back home, no?"

"It's about as close as I've ever tasted. Yeah."

"By da way, she'll be tellin' fortunes tomorrow," he adds, as if to entice me.

He knows I'm not a believer in his voodoo stuff, and fortune telling is not one of the myriad things I admire about his wife. It's weird that he would even bring that up. I'm pondering that, as we continue to walk down the beaten path, when I suddenly become aware of the sound of the steel drums of calypso music wafting down the lane from Port Lucine. Nessie's saloon sounds more lively than usual this afternoon.

I smile at the thought. The sweet rhythmic beat of the drums and the melodic diction of the local singers is one of the many things I love about living in the Caribbean. But Nessie's is even more important to me for another reason. It's also where Trixie Faye sings most evenings. The Hungarian song-bird has roped the hearts of almost every red-blooded male on the island. Mine, more than anyone else's. And I don't mind telling anyone who asks, either.

"So?"

The Candyman's question rips me from my thoughts.

"Huh?" Not sure what he's asking.

"Will you come tomorrow night?" He repeats. "Me'd love to 'ave you. But Angelique even more so." He pauses, eyeing me up and down. "If me were a jealous person, you'd be in *real* trouble."

I chuckle alongside him as we pass through Port Lucine's old wooden gates. They're the only reminder of the large stone wall that once wrapped around the town—and its slave market—to protect itself from the occasional native uprising back when the island was still in its infancy.

"Sure, I'll be there. Lookin' forward to seeing that beautiful missus of yours." I wink at him. "And maybe a shot or two of her apple pie?"

The big man guffaws, shaking his head. "Of course. Of course. I'll be sure to tell her to prepare some for you."

"I'm assuming she won't be too upset about Monday confiscating our score?" I have to ask. It's been a burning question in my gut since leaving the *Dream*.

He shakes his head. "Not at you, she won't. Never at you." A low growl grumbles up from his gut. "It's Mr. Renot what should be worried, when she hears. I would not want to be 'im when she next contacts da *loa*."

The loa. The spirit gods of voodoo. Just as Jacques is a high priest of the voodoo congregation on the island, Angelique is the *mamba*...the high priestess. From all accounts, her magic is supposed to be plenty powerful, if you believe that sort of thing.

He stops just as we reach the entrance of *Nessie's Saloon and Inn*. "Now, I'm assuming d'at d'is is where you get off. I hear a very lovely lady be in there, pining for a handsome sea captain to come home. Don't wanna keep her waitin' no longer." He pulls out a wad of cash and stuffs it down my shirt pocket. Payment for the cargo I've just brought him.

"Wait, no. I can't accept this." I retrieve the money and try to hand it back to him.

"Why not?"

"Because I didn't deliver the goods. I don't deliver, I don't get paid. That's the way it works."

"Seems to me, you *did* deliver da goods, as you say. It was sittin' on St. Noel for a sum total of ten minutes maybe. Not your fault my brother is a backstabbing snake." He pokes me in the chest with an index finger the size of a potato. "No, you keep it. You earned it fair and square, my friend."

I know better than to argue. It would insult him. Besides,

his mind is already made up. I smile a silent thanks. In response, he merely gestures toward the saloon's entrance. "I see you tomorrow, my friend."

Without waiting for a response, he turns toward his candy shop and begins waddling his way there, leaving me in the street and feeling anxious about seeing my girl. Actually, 'my girl' is a bit of a misnomer. You might as well call the ocean, 'my sea,' or the mountain, 'my hill.' Trixie is no one's girl. She's an untamed elemental in her own right. A wild steed that no man could master. I'm just lucky enough to be liked by her more than any other man in these parts. She tolerates me. Even, I suppose, misses me when I'm away. And that alone is enough to get my heart pumping like mad just thinking about it.

Taking a deep breath, I move up the two steps to the saloon's swinging doors and step though. The calypso music washes over me, mixing with the smell of rum, tobacco smoke, and urine. The squawk of the old macaw that Nessie keeps near the entrance overpowers the steel drums, threatening to deafen me. Moe, still perched on my shoulder, turns to the bird and growls, compelling it to lift its wing and hide its beautifully colored face.

"Good job, buddy," I say to the monkey, as I make my way to the bar.

The place is, as I suspected, crowded for late afternoon. Although most work in the sugar cane fields will be done for the day, crowds like this rarely gather until well after sunset during the week. I glance around, returning a few nods and waves as I pass. I'm thankful that most everyone in here seems to be having a good time.

I step up to a bar stool and lean forward, catching Nessie's eye. She's one of the oldest women on St. Noel, at almost sixty-six years of age. She's been running the bar—the only legitimate drinking house that hasn't been taxed out of existence—since her father passed, two decades ago. She never married, but something tells me she would have made a fine wife and a mother, because she's earned a reputation for being a mother to everyone on the island at one point or another. Including me. Truth is, though I'm mighty fond of Angelique Lagrange—the Candyman's wife—this little, bent, old woman, now looking at me, is the closest thing I've had to a mom since my own died, before the war.

"Oh, I see yer finally back, child," she says, showing me the few existing teeth still in her head. "Did you 'ave a good trip?"

She doesn't bother to ask me what I want. She simply bends down behind the counter and returns with an unmarked bottle of rum. She keeps it specifically for her favorite customers, and she pours its golden contents into a glass for me.

I sit down on the stool and watch as she prepares the drink for me, adding various spices to create the concoction with no name that I love so much.

"It was a decent trip," I say, lighting up another cigar while she works. "Went to Miami for a days before I needed to be in Cuba. Caught the Cincinnati Redlegs in a pre-season ball game, which is always nice. Haven't smelled the fresh cut of a baseball diamond in a couple of years. It was like being a kid again."

Nessie just smiles, nodding her head as she listens, then she pushes my drink across the bar to me. "You know, little Malik tells me you plannin' on teaching him and da ot'er kids about da game. Says they even formin' d'eir own league. D'at boy's so excited…"

A ruckus begins to kick up behind me, drawing my attention away from the old lady. The calypso drums peter out, and a hush sweeps over the entire bar. I swivel on my stool, taking in the room as I move. I don't have to look for too long, as my eye quickly catches sight of a blonde whirlwind in the back of the saloon, surrounded by three sharply dressed men.

"Stop being fresh!" Trixie Faye shouts, slapping one of the men across the cheek. The impact seems to sting almost every man in the room, who all cringe from the sound of it. "I said I don't want to dance with you!"

Then, another of the men grabs at her wrists, mumbling something in an accent so thick, it makes it hard to translate from across the room. But his tone speaks volumes, and I don't like it one bit.

I lean my shoulder to one side, and Moe climbs down and scampers across the bar to a perch near the kitchen door. I then glance over at Nessie, who nods her understanding of what I'm about to do. It won't be the first fracas this old tavern's seen, and it won't be the last, I'm sure. But I hate the damage that such things cause to sweet Nessie's little home away from home.

With a sigh, I slide from my stoop and stalk toward the three rudely behaving gentlemen. Though I'm not aware of it consciously, my hands ball up into fists. By the time I reach the man who's grabbing Trixie, I'm already reared back. My fist comes with no warning at all, slugging the creep across the right jaw. He stumbles backward into the chair he'd been occupying before Trixie walked by. His momentum and his weight dash the poor chair to toothpicks, but I don't have time to worry about the damage. Instead, I prepare myself for his closest buddy, who's lunging at me with rage in his eyes.

As he gets close enough, he swings at me, but I lean out of range, just in time. I take hold of Trixie's wrist and spin her out of harm's way, like a man twirling his partner out from him in a waltz. It's a distraction I shouldn't have allowed myself. The first guy, his cheek bright red from Trixie's smack, dives at me, tackling me to the floor. The back of my head comes down hard against the wood, and my ears ring like the bells of Notre Dame. I'm going to have a swell goose egg on my noggin in the morning, but I don't care. These guys have now royally ticked me off.

The guy who tackled me is pounding at my face and my gut with all his might. I hear Trix yelling at him to stop, but he doesn't seem to care what she wants at the moment. I take the pounding, biding my time and letting him wear himself out. If there's one thing boxer Jammin' Jim Thacker's boy knows what to do, it's take a punch.

I glance around the bar from the floor. Everyone's now on their feet, watching and waiting. They all have my back, I know. If it gets too serious, they'll intervene. For now, they're just enjoying the show.

And it's time to give them one they won't soon forget.

When the man on top of me rears back for another punch, throwing himself slightly off balance, I buck up, hurling him to the side. I roll to my left, climbing to my feet in a single motion, and I crouch down with my dukes up near my face in a defensive position.

But one of them is ready for me. The man throws a haymaker at my head before I can blink. Fortunately, I'm faster, and I raise my left arm up to block before immediately throwing up my right leg and kicking him where the sun doesn't shine. He buckles over, holding his family apples and struggling to breathe.

Hey, in a barroom brawl where it's three against one, a fella's got to play dirty if he hopes to get out in one piece, right?

The other two have similar ideas about fair play. The guy I threw off me slips in from behind, grabbing my arms and holding me up. His remaining pal moves in with a one-two punch to my right kidney.

I wheeze, sucking in air. The pain would have doubled me over, if I wasn't being held upright by the lug in the three-piece suit.

"Keep him still," the one that just punched me says. I recognize the accent. I've flown with a handful of Russian pilots a few times during the war. I'd recognize their stilted cadence anywhere.

They're stinking Reds.

The goon holding me pulls me back toward him, tightening his grip, just as his partner moves in for another series of punches. But before the flurry of fists find their mark against my gut, there's a tinkling *thunk* behind me. I'm suddenly free, and I jump out of the way, just as the blow would have connected. His fist pounds into the guy who'd been holding me, just as he's dropping to the floor. I look over to see Trixie standing awkwardly while holding a beer bottle in her hand like a club. She winks at me with spitfire in her eyes. She apparently whacked my captor good with it, and he was already in la-la land before his partner's punch landed in his gut.

And that just leaves one functioning creep to finish off, before this brawl is concluded. I turn toward him, but before the two of us can charge each other, we're interrupted by the shrill screech of a whistle piercing through the roars of excitement in the crowd. We stop and turn toward the saloon's entrance, where a duo of khaki-uniformed police officers—two of the three lawmen who work on St. Noel—stands with hands on their hips, staring us down with disapproving glares.

"Ah, crap," I mumble, stepping back from my opponent, while wiping my bloody nose with my jacket's sleeve.

The remaining Red looks at me with questioning eyes. He

can obviously tell the difference in my demeanor has shifted from confident brawler to compliant suspect. Of course, if he knew how much Chief Armad hates me—hates any 'white devils' who visits his island, really—he'd understand. Last thing I need is the local constabulary to get involved in all this.

"Well, well, well," one of the officers says, as he moves through the parting crowd with his hands behind his back. His name is Marvin Conard, the second senior officer of the force. He's not nearly as ambitious as the Chief, but he's got his own quirks that spell trouble for guys like me. "If it ain't da famous Captain Joe, in da flesh. Back from his big trip to Havana." He stops in front of me and offers a series of 'Tsks' in my direction. "Should 'ave stayed there, if you want me unsolicited advice."

The other two men in suits have finally picked themselves up off the floor and gathered around the third in a protective huddle. They're glaring at me and ignoring the coppers, as if they have no qualms about the law at all.

Which makes me even more nervous about my situation.

I remember what Monday told me about the Russians. They're guests of the Governor. He even set them up in some rooms at Nessie's inn—free of charge.

"Crap, crap, crap," I mutter, rolling my eye as I stare up into the ceiling. They're not afraid of Marvin and his young partner, Lloyd Gano, because they're protected here. They can do pretty much anything they want, and they won't have to answer to anyone other than the Governor.

"Okay, Marvin," I start to say, while holding up my hands. "I see what this looks like, but…"

"They were harassing me," Trixie suddenly speaks up, slipping between me and the copper, with her hands firmly on her exquisitely curved hips. "They grabbed me. Joe here was just looking out for me. He was just being my knight in shining armor. That's all."

Her eyes burn like lava at the police officer, challenging him to arrest me. I stare at her in awe. If Jayne Mansfield had a prettier twin sister, who had the fierceness and fortitude of Katherine Hepburn, it would be Trixie. Not many people on the island would ever dare cross her, and I know Marvin will be no exception.

"If you want to arrest someone, arrest them!" she says, pointing at the three Russians.

Officer Marvin's eyes drift down to his shoes, unwilling to look her in the eyes and duty-bound to ignore her accusations toward the Russians. His partner, a youngster really, whose qualifications came down to the fact that the uniform fit him, stands back. His eyes are wide with uncertainty, but he's already made up his mind not to anger Trixie any further.

Smart boy.

"Don't be ridiculous," one of the Reds says. "We are guests on your island." The man who went to town on my kidney, points at me. "I demand you arrest this man, this instant. He assaulted us unprovoked. Without warning. It was most unsporting of him."

I turn and glower at him. "Look, Ivan, where I come from, a man doesn't try to force a lady to dance when they don't want to. And your *comrade* there..." I nod to his friend on the right while emphasizing the word 'comrade' with as much contempt as possible. "...just took it one step too far, when he grabbed her wrists."

Someone quietly clears a soft feminine throat, but the entire crowd grows stock still at the sound. Each of us turn toward the bar, where Nessie stands, a shotgun the size of an elephant gun gripped tight in her little hands.

"Gentlemen, if you please," Nessie says. Her brows are arched at a jagged angle above her eyes. "Dis is me establishment, and I expect you all to settle down." She nods at Marvin and his partner. "Ain't no serious crimes been committed here tonight. Ain't no need for your services here, neither. So, be on your way and leave d'ese boys to me. I'll see to d'em good and proper."

One look in her eyes and everyone in the room can tell she means every word of it, too. And my legal troubles just ambled out the door like dogs with their tails between their legs.

CHAPTER 3

Although the coppers have gone, I'm by no means out of the woods yet. There is still the matter of Nessie's wrath to contend with, though I'm pretty sure it's only the Reds that have anything to truly worry about.

Moving around the bar, still leveling her double-barreled shotgun at us, she eases herself across the saloon. Her withering stare never falters from the Russians, and she moves, catlike, toward us. When she's within five feet of us, she stops.

"I typically don't mind none if some of my patrons get a little rowdy in me bar," she says, looking from one man to the next, including myself. "But when yer antics draw the attention of da law, d'at's where I draw da line."

She looks over at Trixie. "You all right, child?"

The songbird smiles, then nods.

Nessie looks over at me. "You about as sharp as a box of the Candyman's gumballs, ain't ya, boy?" She shakes her head. "Takin' on t'ree of d'em on your own, knowin' full well Trixie can handle herself just fine wit'out you."

Though I'm not aware I'm doing it, my head scrunches down into my shoulders, like a scolded kid getting reamed by his granny. She stares at me for another moment, then nods back toward the door.

"Go on home now, child," she says to me. "I'll deal wit' d'ese 'friends' of da Governor and smooth t'ings over nice and good."

I know better than to argue. Turning, I move over to the bar, where Moe quickly finds his perch on my shoulder again, and I walk out the swinging doors while nursing my swelling lip. As I leave, I can hear Nessie lecturing the Russians so bad it would have made Hitler himself run with his tail between his legs.

I smile at the thought, as I dust off my captain's cap and light up another cigar outside the saloon. Nessie is right. It's been a long day for me, and the best place for me to go is back to the *Dream* and get some shuteye. It certainly seems to be the safest plan at the moment. But I came to Nessie's to see Trixie, and I haven't even been able to have a single quiet moment with her ruby red lips. To me, that's just not fair at all.

I hear the saloon doors squeak and the soft tread of dainty feet on the bamboo porch behind me. I turn to see Trixie Faye herself, smiling down at me from the step.

"Howdy, cowboy," she says, giving me a wink. The dress she's wearing would be illegal back in the States. Red sequins cover most of the fabric. The fabric, however, leaves little to the imagination, with its low-cut design and a slit that runs from the hem of the dress up to her upper thigh.

I can only stare back at her, trying to find the right words.

"Um, hi," I finally say. Not exactly Shakespearean, but it's the best I can do at the moment.

Her hands behind her back, she steps down from the porch demurely, and strolls over to me. When she's within a handful of inches away, she steps on her tiptoes and plants a heavenly kiss right on my lips. My legs feel like jelly from the warm contact.

"I just wanted to say thank you," she says when the kiss is over. Though born in Budapest, she lived in New York City since she was thirteen. Her Hungarian accent has all but disappeared in the fifteen years since. "Nessie's right. I could've handled them just fine, but it's always nice to know my knight is there to watch out for me, when the time comes."

I'm pretty sure I'm blushing when she reaches up, takes me in her arms, and kisses me again. This time, harder. More passionate. I return the passion, enjoying the heat that radiates against both of us as we embrace. We stay like that for several minutes, entwined in each other's arms. The steel drums of the calypso band has already begun their melodic beat again, meaning that Nessie must have diffused the situation as she promised. But at the moment, I don't care. The only thing that matters is the soft, warm curves of Trixie's waist in my hands, and her wet lips pressed against my own.

Finally, she pulls away. I try to hold on to her, but she laughs and thumbs back at the saloon. "Sorry, Captain, but it's almost time for my show." She kisses my cheek and backs away. "Will I see you tomorrow night?"

"Tomorrow night?"

She rolls her eyes. "The festival, you big lug."

"Oh, yeah. Right. The festival." I nod. "Sure, yeah. I'll be around."

She backs up the steps, beaming from ear to ear, then tucks a strand of her golden hair behind her ear, gives me a wave, and turns into the saloon without another word. I stand there watching her disappear into the smoke-filled bar and sigh, while gently touching my lips where she'd kissed them.

She's quite a woman. No wonder everyone in town is nuts about her.

With her gone and no other reason to stay, I turn toward the town gates and start making my way back to the dock and my boat—the second love of my life. My bed most definitely is calling me, and I look forward to a good night's rest.

I casually stroll down the dirt road, enjoying my stogie as I gaze up into the star-filled canopy of the night sky. The view is hampered by the dense jungle vegetation of the island, but the deep blues and purples mixing with the silver pinpricks of light that stretch above the trees is mesmerizing.

The sound of Trixie's angelic singing is carried by the wind, and I'm only half aware of where I'm going as I move along the path. Moe, for his part, seems oblivious to the tranquil beauty of it all and, instead, zips from one tree to the next in playful leaps.

It's a gorgeous night. The reason I moved to the Caribbean in the first place. If not for the throbbing pain of my lip and the knot on the back of my head from the fight a few minutes ago, it would be near perfection. So perfect, in fact, that I almost don't catch sight of the furtive figure moving a few yards ahead of me. The figure—very much of the masculine variety —dashes from the trees on the side of the road to my right, toward the left. He's quick. Stealthy. If not for the silver light of the crescent moon above, I might not have seen him at all.

I reach into the inside of my jacket and pull my .45. Moe, seeing the gun, leaps back around my neck, preparing for action.

I stop. "Did you see him, too?" I whisper to the monkey.

Moe looks at me, cocks his head, and begins scratching at the fleas behind his ear.

"Lot of good you are."

Cautiously, I step forward, keeping my gun trained dead ahead. For all I know, it could be one of the kids on the island playing games with me. But the way things have gone today,

I'm not so sure. Strange things are going down in St. Noel. The feud between the Candyman and his brother. Monday's sudden interest in my business. And those three Reds who are getting a free stay at Nessie's.

It's the Russians that make me more nervous than anything. The way they hold themselves...their clothing and their military demeanor... It reeks of government men to me. KGB, maybe? I've heard lots of reports recently about how they've taken an interest in the Caribbean because of the islands' close proximity to the United States. They've been stirring up trouble here and there, drumming up the dissatisfied masses in hopes of rebellion—and in the hopes of the islanders welcoming the communist way into their lives. The very thought of that happening here in St. Noel is almost laughable, though. Capitalism is alive and well here. And though many of the inhabitants are poor by Western standards, most are very content with what they have.

I'm strolling again, keeping my eyes peeled for any sudden movements. Concern over the Russians right now is silly. They're still back at the saloon. No way they could have gotten ahead of me and set up some sort of ambush without me seeing them. There could be more of them, but Monday specifically said there were only three. So, whoever just dashed out in front of me, was probably someone else entirely.

Monday, maybe?

He got shown his place earlier today, and I can see him wanting to pay me a visit after his encounter with the Candyman. But the shadowy figure was far too thin to be the obese customs agent. Plus, by now, Monday's probably too knee-deep in rum or gin to really be much of a threat. And he's definitely not as stealthy as that shadow was.

I'm now about a half a mile from the dock. The same distance behind me leads to town. The silky voice of Trixie

Faye is now barely audible. The jungle is still, except for the occasional breeze that nudges the palm fronds and mangrove leaves around. There're no animal sounds of any kind, making me even more tense.

Something's just not right.

"You gonna use that peashooter, or you just like strokin' it like a security blanket?"

The voice came from behind me. I wheel around, my finger tightening on the .45 as I move. A halo of light from Port Lucine blocks my view of the man. I take aim and prepare to fire.

"Whoa, whoa, whoa!" The man raises his arms, waving his hands in the air to reveal he's unarmed. "Is that anyway to treat an old friend, JoeJoe?"

I lower the gun, and my heart skips a beat. Only one man I know ever called me 'JoeJoe.' And he only did it because he knew how much I hate it.

I squint in his direction, trying to see his face, despite the backlight behind him. I don't know why I bothered. Although I can't see his face for squat, my one eye can't help but take in the gaudy Hawaiian shirt covering his tall, lanky frame. That's all I need to confirm my suspicions are true. This guy wore the brightest, most God-awful floral print shirts religiously—almost like they were a badge of courage or something. They were, in many ways, his calling card, I guess you could say.

"Morris? Morris Grant, is that you?" I step closer, and his usual clean-shaven, rakish face comes into view.

He's smiling at me, though his hands are still raised for dear life.

Lieutenant Morris Grant, US Navy Intelligence. We met during the war and became thick as thieves from that day on. I even named the monkey, Moe, after him. But we haven't seen each other since the Allies declared victory and the Nazis were sent running to whatever dark hole they could find.

I holster my gun and take him in a tight bear hug. He claps my back a few times before gently pushing me away. His smile dissolves.

"Look, we can't talk here. Now." He shoots furtive glances over his shoulders, before continuing. "I'm in a bit of a pickle."

I laugh. "When the hell aren't you?"

"I'm serious, JoeJoe. Big time serious. And I need your help." He sidesteps a few feet to his left, moving back into the shadows of the nighttime jungle. "Too many busybodies around now."

I glance around. As far as I can tell, there's no one around for at least half a mile. But the look on his face tells me everything. My old friend is scared. And given his reputation for being fearless on and off the battlefield, that's enough to make me stand to attention and take notice.

"I'll reach out to you soon," he says. He's already invisible within the vegetation. "Don't tell a soul you've seen me, okay? Not until I can explain what's going on." He pauses. "Just watch your back, JoeJoe. Those commies you tussled with, back at the saloon? They mean business."

Was he at Nessie's? Did he see the fight?

"I'll be in touch," he repeats, and then he disappears from sight completely.

CHAPTER 4

I didn't sleep a wink all night. My head is still buzzing with the million questions raised by my old buddy's sudden and mysterious return into my life—and just how the three Ruskies fit into it all.

I've tossed and turned throughout the night, getting up here and there for a few fingers of rum just to soothe my nerves. The sun is now inching its orange-red haze above the horizon, and I'm sitting on the upper deck of the *Dream*, still trying to sort it all out while eating a plate of scrambled eggs and coffee.

I'm taking a sip from my steaming mug when the familiar, yet unwelcome petite figure of police Chief Fidel Armad strolls past the pier's chain-link gate and bounds down the gangplank onto the dock. He's alone, which I suppose, is a good sign for me. He's not prone to officiate arrests without his goons as backup.

I watch him saunter down the dock, his nose turned imperiously toward the rising sun. His coffee-hued skin glistens with sweat, even in the early morning hours. When he comes to a stop at the bow of the *Dream*, his jaundiced eyes turn toward me and he greets me with a sneer.

"Captain Thacker." He nods a greeting.

I lift my coffee cup in replied. "Chief."

He sniffs. "I understand you caused quite a ruckus in Nessie's last night."

I shrug. "Depends on who you ask. All but three will say they started it when they manhandled Trixie the way they did." I finish the last bit of eggs on my plate and wash it down. "Besides, Nessie isn't pressing charges."

I could be nicer to the pint-sized chief, but he's rubbed me the wrong way since Day One. He's never been a fan of outsiders to his island, and he generally makes life miserable for anyone of European descent who comes to St. Noel. He's also a racist, plain and simple, and I don't particularly like racists of any kind. That's just the way my mama raised me to be.

"That's fine. That's fine." Though a native of the island, Armad spent a great deal of his youth abroad. He's all but lost his Caribbean accent, which somehow makes him even more unlikeable to me. "I'm not here about that, Thacker. Not here about that at all."

I finish off my coffee and lean back in my lawn chair, waiting for him to continue. After a moment, he clears his throat.

"I'm here because I've been made aware of an unregistered visitor to the island."

I stiffen at the statement, but hope he doesn't notice.

"An unregistered...um, what?"

"Visitor," he repeats. "Someone who has sneaked onto St. Noel without documentation. An American, by all accounts."

"Er, okay." I shrug. "So why come to me?"

Armad huffs impatiently. "Well, you're the only other American on the island…"

"So, you think I must know the guy, is that it? Tell me, Fidel… You're from the Caribbean. Do you know Carl, who runs the bait shop on the beach on St. Thomas?"

The chief rolls his eyes. "That's not what I was implying. But you do often charter your boat out for tours and such. I've come to see if this man has approached you."

He holds out a piece of paper. I whistle, drawing Moe's attention. When the monkey comes above deck, I point to the paper and mutter an indecipherable command. In a flash, he leaps down from the bow to the dock, scurries up Armad's tiny leg, and takes the paper from his hand. Then the monkey brings it up to me.

Intentionally taking my sweet time, I light up a cigar and take a few puffs before unfolding the paper and giving it a good once over. As I suspected, a black and white, hazy image of my old war buddy, Morris Grant, stares back at me. I read the print underneath the picture:

WANTED
For questioning in regards suspicion of espionage and other illegal activities.
Morris Alan Grant, DOB: July 27, 1914
United States Citizen, Affiliation unknown.
Considered armed and dangerous. Report him to your local constabulary if sighted.
Do not approach.

ESPIONAGE? While Morris had been involved in intelligence operations while in the Navy, he'd retired when the war ended. Last I heard, he was working at his father's furniture store, back in Virginia. I'm not sure what kind of trouble he's currently in—Lord knows he has the propensity to grift whenever and wherever he has the chance, which got him in more hot water than I can hope to remember back in the Philippines—but I can't imagine him being mixed up in espionage anymore. When the war ended, he couldn't wait to get out of government service and return home to his ma and pa.

After a moment, I look back at Chief Armad and shake my head. "Sorry. Haven't seen him around." I point to the picture. "So, what's he done anyway? He some kind of spy or something?"

I hope my natural curiosity doesn't draw too much suspicion, but I figure it's a natural line of questioning that anyone might ask.

"Right now, all I can say is that he's on the island illegally. Snuck in somehow." His eyes narrow as he makes a show of examining my boat. Like Monday Renot, he's fully aware of my smuggling operation. It's actually not surprising he might suspect me of sneaking Morris onto the island. It's something I would have done without a second thought, actually.

"Before you say anything, no. I didn't smuggle him here," I say. "Like I said, I haven't seen the fella." I show Armad my teeth, with a Cheshire grin. "But if I do, you'll be the first to know. Scout's honor."

"Oh, I know how much you care about your civic duty, Captain Thacker." His polite smile appears as more of a sneer than anything else. "Just remember. The Governor has his eyes on you, and he has threatened more than a few times to deport you from our island. Just remember that when you start to wonder where your loyalties lie."

"Like I said, Chief. I don't know this man from Adam." I hold up the Wanted poster. "I've got no loyalty issues to worry about."

He nods, then turns to walk away.

"Just remember to let us know if you see him," Armad says, as he trudges along the wooden pier, walks through the gate, and disappears up the path heading toward town.

Moe whimpers as we watch the Chief go. I give the monkey a good scratch behind his ear, then mash my cigar into the ashtray on the table, and let out a nervous breath. I'm not sure what kind of trouble Morris is in, but I've already decided that I don't like it one bit.

CHAPTER 5

The Candyman's festival is already in full swing when I make my way up the mile-long hike from my boat to town. I've left Moe at the *Dream*. Festivals like this tend to end with massive fireworks displays, and the little monkey is ridiculously scared of loud booms. I figure he's better off back at the boat, where he can hide under the pile of dirty clothes near my bed until I get back.

The streets are lit with myriad colored paper lanterns hanging from twine along the lamp posts throughout the village. From the looks of things, the entire island appears to be present, wearing papier-mâché masks depicting devils and the dead, and dancing a merry jig up and down the town's streets. The distinct odor of alcohol permeates the air, mixing sweetly with the scent of the recently blooming island flowers that paint the nearby vegetation in hues of red, yellow, and purple.

A makeshift stage has been constructed in front of Nessie's saloon, where a calypso band sings tunes by Louis Jordan and Harry Belafonte to everyone's delight. Children of all ages, dressed in spooky costumes of every sort, dash back and forth through the streets, searching for candy hidden in the most devious places by the Candyman.

I smile as I take it all in. To me, it's just another example of what it means to live in paradise. An entire community coming together to enjoy each others' company. Fun. Music. Dancing. And if one is really lucky, maybe a little lovemaking, to boot.

With that thought in mind, my neck cranes as I search the crowd for Trixie Faye. It's a relatively simple task to pick out her golden locks among the throng of black curls, as people dance their hearts out. It takes less than two seconds to find her, near Jimmy Gernot's Apothecary. My cheeks flush as I watch her smile casually at someone, and I find myself wishing it was me.

Then, I do a double take. I've just seen who she's smiling at. It's a well-dressed man with dark hair in a Brooks Brother's tweed suit. One of the Reds from yesterday. I clench my fist and take a step forward, but stop myself. Trixie doesn't appear to be in distress. She's simply talking with the creep. Seems amicable enough, though her eyes keep darting back and forth from time to time as they chat.

My insides begin to boil with a simmering jealousy, which is crazy. First, I'm not that kind of guy. I'm not the jealous type at all. Second, Trixie would never go for a commie. She left that life behind years ago, when her parents fled the Soviet regime. She has no love for the USSR or for anyone who'd work for them. Trixie is all American now. And third, it's a party. People are supposed to put aside their differences and enjoy chatting people up at shindigs like this.

But mostly, I tamp down my jealousy because if I act on it and my hackles get raised in front of her, Trixie will never let me live it down. She also might not forgive me, since, as she's told me on numerous occasions, she's 'no one's girl.'

That being said, I do feel it's prudent to approach her. Might be a nice gesture to try to make peace with the Russian, too. You know. International relations and all that. After all, if Trixie can put aside her differences over the way he and his boys treated her last night, I should be able to as well.

I start wading through the crowd, making as straight a line as I can to the apothecary. After a few halts to say hello here and there, as well as to return a ball to one of the kids, I finally make it. Trixie's smile widens when she sees me, and she immediately plunges into my arms with a full hug. When we separate, I look past her shoulders and prepare to greet our Russian guest, but he's nowhere to be seen.

I crane my head, looking for him.

"Where'd he go?" I ask.

"Where'd who go?"

"The guy you were just talking to. That Russian."

She takes a look behind her and turns back to me. "Oh, he's gone. I've no idea where he's gotten himself off to."

My eye is still scanning the crowd, but it's as though the Red simply ghosted away.

"Why Captain Joe, you aren't jealous, are you?" She giggles.

"Of course not. Don't be ridiculous." I adjust my cap across my forehead and try to look shocked at the mere suggestion. "I just wanted to bury the hatchet. That's all."

Trixie shrugs. "That might be more difficult than you'd like."

A boy dressed in clean white pants and a shirt saunters up to us, carrying a silver tray topped with an assortment of alcoholic beverages. I take a glass of whiskey on ice. Trixie chooses a flute of Champagne, and the boy moves off into the crowd once more.

"Why do you say that? About being difficult to bury the hatchet, I mean."

"Well, he certainly isn't your biggest fan," she laughs, taking a sip of the sparkling drink. "And he was definitely curious about you, too. Asking all sorts of questions about you and your friends."

I stiffen. "Friends? What friends?"

"Oh, just friends. He was particularly interested in some of your old war buddies. Asked if any of them ever came around to visit."

So the Red is looking for Morris. Definitely not good.

"So, what did you tell him?"

She finishes her Champagne and laughs again. "What was I supposed to tell him? You rarely ever talk about the war. And when you do, I figure over half of the stories are made up. I told him I don't have a clue who any of your friends are—except those on St. Noel, that is."

Someone sets off a rope of firecrackers nearby.

Pop-pop-pop-pow-pop-bang-bang!

I jump, nearly spilling my whiskey.

"Geez, Joe." Trixie reaches out a hand and strokes the stubble of my cheeks. Her soft touch sends a wave of electricity through my nerves. "You're awfully jumpy tonight. What's wrong?"

I shake my head. "I'm not sure." I return my attention to the crowd, but there's no sign of a suit anywhere in the vicinity. "But I don't trust those Reds. At all."

"Oh, pish-posh." She waves my concern away with her hands. "They're not spies or anything...if that's what you're thinking. Boris—that's the guy I was just talking to, Boris Usilov. He told me they are actually anthropologists. From the University of Moscow. They've come to the islands for some research. They're bookworms, Joe. Nothing more."

She didn't feel how hard they hit last night. Didn't notice their military bearing and skill.

Anthropologists, my right toe.

"Joe!" I hear someone shouting to me from the mass of costumed people. I turn around and it doesn't take me long to see the monstrous form of Jacque 'The Candyman' Lagrange making his way toward us. He's dressed as Baron Samedi, the chief loa of the dead, with a black top hat, painted face to resemble a skull, and a black tuxedo. He's not wearing a shirt under the tuxedo jacket, but a full set of skeletal ribs has been painted across his chest and down his immense belly. As he takes the steps up to the apothecary's porch, he pulls me into a bear hug that threatens to crack at least three of my vertebrae. A moment later, he puts me back on solid ground, pats both my shoulders with his bear claws for hands, and smiles over at Trixie. "My Lord, girl, you are lookin' more lovely every time I see you."

Trixie blushes, dipping her head in a miniature curtsy, and offers him her hand. The Candyman brushes the hand away and draws her into a slightly less hearty, yet just as enthusiastic embrace.

"Joe, when you gonna make an honest woman out d'is songbird, mon? You better sweep her up fast, before da rest of da island gets da courage to do it."

I laugh, raising an eyebrow at Trixie as I do so. "Trust me, pal. I'd run to the church right now, if she let me."

Trixie giggles at us. "Oh, stop it you two. You're embarrassing me."

The three of us chat for a few minutes, watching the crowd enjoying the festivities all around us. I finish my glass of whiskey and sit it down on a nearby table. I'm just beginning to withdraw a cigar when the Candyman excuses himself from Trixie and pulls me aside.

"Don't light up just yet, my friend." His eyes seem to twinkle in the multicolored lantern light around us. "Angelique sent me out here to find you. She says it's time to tell you your fortune."

I look up into his big skull-painted face and roll my eye. "Come on, Jacques," I say. "I mean no offense, but you know I don't buy all your voodoo mum..." He glares down at me, a silent warning to choose my next words carefully. "...er, I mean, your voodoo beliefs. It's just not my thing. You're talking to a Baptist boy, born and raised."

His death-head grin spreads with a raucous laugh that seems to shake the wooden walkway under our feet. "Don't matter none if *you* believe or not, Joe. A meetin' wit' Angelique is a rare honor indeed. Whether your future is told you or not, Mama Lagrange wants to spend some time wit' her favorite white boy on da island. You gonna disappoint her?"

I shake my head. "Of course not." And I mean it. Although I'm not overly fond of all the superstitious nonsense the islanders around her believe, Angelique Lagrange is an angel in human flesh. While Nessie has taken on the role of doting grandmother since I came to St. Noel, Angelique is something of a loving and nurturing aunt. I adore her, and I feel guilty for neglecting her for as long as I have. The least I can do is play along with her delusions of psychic powers and spend some good quality time with her. "Okay, Jacques. Let's go."

I say goodbye to Trixie, being sure to set up a time and place for us to meet later tonight, and I follow the big man as we stroll past the revelers and move past his shop. A line of excited children forms out the door, waiting for old man Guillermo, the Candyman's loyal store clerk, to hand out the new stock of treats to them for a penny a piece. I wave at Malik, waiting patiently near the back of the line. As he waits, he tosses a baseball up into the air, and catches it with his mitt.

We pass the candy store, moving around the side of the building, toward the Candyman's family bungalow in back. The lively sounds of more music and revelry can be heard from the cellar below the store. I know the Candyman's private speakeasy is probably even more boisterous than the activities outdoors. I kind of regret not having time to go down and share in a few pints with a few of my friends, but Angelique needs to come first.

"Any idea what's so important that she's insisting on seeing me?" I ask as we round the corner of the store. His villa is directly behind it, richly decorated in the same lanterns that paint the rest of the town in a rainbow of light.

"Does she need a reason, boy? She loves you like a son."

I nod, offering him a silent apology.

"But to answer your question, no. I've no idea what's got her bonnet all twisted for you lately. Da moment she heard word you were pullin' in to port, she sent me down to da pier to escort da cargo back."

That bit of news sets me on edge. Like I said earlier, while the Candyman is the face and muscle of the operation, Angelique has always been the brains. If she was concerned about my Cuban run...

"How'd she take the news about Monday taking our crates?"

We're now approaching the villa's front door, and I notice both our voices have lowered to near whispers.

"She was upset, naturally." He shakes his big bald head at me. "But don't worry. She not mad at you. She genuinely worried about you, I t'ink. Besides, she told me to invite you to d'is 'reading' before d'at weasel Monday got his grubby mitts on our shipment. Don't 'ave nothin' to do wit' it at all."

He opens the front door and gestures for me to enter. I move into the large, bamboo-paneled foyer and remove my cap. My muscles have noticeably relaxed with Jacques's reassurances. Besides, Angelique has nothing to worry about. I have every intention of getting that cargo back, and I'm already well on my way to forming a pretty good plan to do it, too.

I've taken a few steps into the home's interior before I realize my companion is not beside me. I turn to see his big skeleton-painted face smiling at me in the doorway.

"Enjoy, my friend."

"Wait. You're not coming?"

He shakes his head. "No, no, no. D'ere's too much fun to be had out here!" He laughs his big burly laugh. "Besides, da invitation was for you alone. It really is quite an honor, no?"

He winks at me before closing the big double doors to his house. If I was anyone else, I might be nervous about being left alone here like this. It has all the earmarks of a setup. But I'm not 'anyone else.' I'm Joe Thacker, and Jacques and Angelique are dear friends. The one thing I know about the way they do business is that friendship and loyalty are far more important to them than money. They could lose millions, but they'd never throw a friend to the wolves. That much, I know without doubt.

With that in mind, I clutch my captain's hat under my arm, and move toward the back of the house, where I know Angelique waits.

CHAPTER 6

When most Americans imagine the residences of voodoo priests, I suppose they picture black-painted rooms, blood-drenched floors, and grass dolls impaled with a number of pins designed to do unspeakable things to unsuspecting victims. Nothing, however, could be farther from the truth. At least, as far as the Lagrange estate is concerned.

The foyer is bright and cheery with pristine white walls and beautiful bamboo floors that cover the entire two-story structure. An odd assortment of statuary—ranging from island deities to Grecian urns—lines much of the walls, except in places covered by bookshelves, hunting trophies, and colorful oil paintings created by Angelique herself.

I step from the foyer into the den—a sunken affair with a plush velvet-covered couch that wraps around a mahogany coffee table in the center of the room. A crystal chandelier hangs above, illuminating everything with warm light.

I stop just short of the plush velvet couch and loveseat, and I look around. I've been here dozens of times. I'm fully aware of where Angelique holds court, and I could easily traverse the house to my destination. But the rules of the house must be maintained. Proper etiquette is essential.

I wait, clearing my throat as loudly as I can to announce my presence.

After a moment, when no one appears, I decide more drastic measures are necessary. "Um, hello? Anyone here?"

I hear the shuffle of feet and a muttered curse from somewhere in the house. The voice is feminine and very young, and I smile. The house maid hasn't been advised of impending guests. I'm not expected by the servants, and now, I've caught them with their proverbial pants down.

The maid scurries into the den, wearing the traditional short black dress of her position. She adjusts her apron, as if she's just gotten out of bed. She puts on her maid's cap over a severe hair bun while muttering apologies for keeping me waiting. She's a lovely caramel-skinned doll with deep brown eyes and a petite and lithe frame. Her eyes are large and doe-like, and she has full pouty lips. Her lipstick is smeared slightly on one side of her mouth, but it doesn't detract at all from her beauty. Although I've never seen her before, I'm certain she turns a lot of heads in town whenever she's off duty.

Heck, she's the epitome of the Candyman's 'type.' I have no doubt it was his idea to hire such a lovely creature for his rather infamous extramarital activities.

"I'm so very sorry," she repeats. Her accent is more French than Caribbean, and I guess she's spent time in France, rather than the islands. Perhaps studying abroad. But her complexion, not to mention her employers, tell me one thing for sure—she's a native of St. Noel. The Candyman and his wife would never hire anyone for domestic duties they couldn't trust, and they rarely ever trust anyone not born on the island.

I wave her apologies away and shake my head. "Nothing

to be sorry about, Doll-face. Why would you expect guests when the real party is going on outside?"

She smiles, obvious relief washing over her lovely face. "You are Captain Joe, *oui*?"

I nod.

"I've heard a great deal about you." She offers a polite curtesy. "The Gentleman and Lady Lagrange talk about you all ze time. As do many people on ze island."

"If they say good things about me, just go ahead and believe the opposite," I say, offering her my most charming smile. "If you hear bad things about me... Well, that you can probably believe."

She laughs at that, adjusts her maid's cap again, and then stares expectantly at me.

"Oh," I say, realizing she has no idea why I'm here. For the life of me, I don't understand why Jacques didn't announce my presence. Then again, the Candyman's been pretty excited about the festival for weeks. His desire to return to the party wasn't a ruse. "Sorry. I believe Mrs. Angelique is expecting me in the parlor. She's invited me to have my fortune told."

The maid's eyes widen in awe. To anyone else on the island, such an invitation is the equivalent of a sit-down with the Pope, an honor of the highest caliber. She soon realizes she's staring at me with admiration, and she blushes. "Excuse me while I go to my mistress and announce your arrival." She gestures toward the other side of the room to a small bar. "Please, make yourself a drink, if you like. I know they wouldn't mind."

I offer a nod of thanks and watch her shapely legs saunter out of the room. Then I make my way over to the bar. I don't want to ruin my appetite for some of Angelique's apple pie, but a small glass of spiced rum never hurt anyone. I search the bottles, pick my favorite label, and pour myself a finger or two of the golden nectar. I down it in one gulp; just in time for the maid to return to the den.

"Madam Lagrange is ready for you now, Captain."

"Thank you, Miss…?"

"Clarise. Just call me Clarise."

I set the glass down at the bar and follow her back to through the hallway she's just come from, until we reach a set of French double doors. A set of red velvet curtains block the view from inside the room beyond. Clarise taps on the door twice, then opens it, and gestures for me to enter.

"Thanks, Darlin'," I say, and I stroll inside. I hear the door shut gently behind me. The ample form of Angelique is sitting in a chair behind a table on the other side of the room. Her eyes are bright, and her smile says she's genuinely pleased to see me. "That's some maid you've got there." I shoot my thumb behind me. "Easy on the eyes."

Angelique laughs. "Clarise is new. Just started two weeks ago, while you were away." She gets up from behind the table and strolls over toward me. For such a robust woman, she moves with the grace and ease of a runway model. "And I thought she might catch your eye." Without further chit-chat, she embraces me in a way that would make her husband seem like a ninety pound weakling, then plants two soft kisses on both my cheeks. I feel her hand brush my bottom as she moves back.

I might have misrepresented my relationship with Angelique earlier. The voodoo mamba is twenty years my senior and easily twice as heavy as me. And while I tell everyone she's like my dear old auntie, she's had her eyes on me for years to be her next little play thing. Always trying to play footsies with me when her husband's not around. It's a game we've come to play, and I can deal with it easily enough because I've grown to truly like the woman she is, when she's not trying to make time with me.

"It's good to see you, Joe. You don't come see me enough, boy... Always gallivantin' 'round in yer silly boat and wit' d'at skinny blonde floozy."

Oh, yeah. I also forgot to mention that Angelique is not a fan of Trixie Faye in the slightest. I've learned to ignore her rants about the Hungarian songstress, out the love and respect I've developed for the mamba.

"Ah, come, Angelique. Don't start that again."

"Never you mind about her right now." She waves for me to take a seat at the table. "Right now is *my* time, not hers. Right now, I got you all to myself."

The smile on her face is outright lascivious.

I walk to the other side of the table and pull the chair out for her. She graciously accepts and sits down, then waits for me to take my seat on the opposite side. Once comfortable, Angelique tugs at a red velvet rope attached to the servant's bell. A moment later, there's another double tap on the door, and Clarise enters the room again, carrying a silver tray with two crystal glasses and a decanter of a brown liquid. A handful of cinnamon sticks are floating in it. The maid sets the tray down on a cart and wheels it next to the table, before silently departing again.

"I believe you were promised some of my apple pie, no?" Angelique is beaming, no doubt at the boyish delight I must have scrawled all across my face. Although I learned the science of moonshining from my grandfather back home, I've never quite perfected the *art* of flavoring it to taste like real apple pie. My mother had become the queen of it, back home in Eubank. Angelique is very serious competition for her crown.

The mamba reaches over and picks up the decanter while I place a glass in front of each of us, being careful to avoid knocking over the crystal ball that acts as a center-piece on the table. For a few minutes, the two of us don't say a word. We simply lean back in our chairs and enjoy the confectionary liquor with great delight. We down the first glass, and then quickly move on to the second and third. My throat is burning, while my tastebuds dance a merry jig in my mouth. But before we risk becoming too inebriated, Angelique's face grows stern. She places the near empty decanter back on the tray and waits for me to finish the last of my glass before she removes it from my reach.

I look at her. Her soft round face has suddenly become hard. Her eyes narrow, and there's a slight wrinkle in her brow I've never seen before. Someone who doesn't know her like I do might think she's furious. I know better. The look she's giving me now has little to do with anger and everything to do with worry.

"Joe, we have a problem," she says without preamble. She reaches over and pulls the servant's bell again. "And it's putting us all in danger."

Well, she certainly has my attention now. If I was feeling any ill effect from the alcohol, it's completely evaporated from my system now.

I'm just about to ask her to explain, when the doors behind me open without the customary knock this time. I turn around, expecting to see Clarise again, but my jaw drops when my old pal Morris Grant struts into the parlor while buttoning up the most horrendously brilliant floral print shirt I've ever had the misfortune to be blinded by. It's bright red with yellow flowers all over it.

First thing that goes through my head when I see Morris is: that little son of a gun is the one who was playing pattycakes with the maid when I first arrived. The second thought that then begins to supersede everything else is…

"Morris? What the heck are you doing here?"

I stand up from the table, glancing from Angelique to my old war buddy. To my knowledge, Morris has never been on St. Noel. There's no way he should know Angelique Lagrange, much less know her well enough to be bebopping the hired help.

The mamba is now standing as well. She gestures over toward Morris. "Joe, may I present to you 'the problem' I was just mentioning."

I look over at my friend, who's giving me an awkward, sheepish smile. "Told you we'd talk soon, JoeJoe," he says, moving over to the table and taking a third seat. Angelique and I take our original places at the table, but I keep looking between them both, waiting for an explanation. I don't have to wait long.

"Joe, dear, I'm about to tell you somet'ing not even Jacques knows about me," Angelique begins. "I work for *Service de Documentation Extérieure et de Contre-Espionnage*."

"You're a French spy?" My voice is louder than anyone in the room would prefer, but the news is a shock. The idea that Angelique Lagrange—voodoo priestess and lifelong resident of St. Noel, is a spy for the SDECE is beyond my wildest imaginings.

"And *I* work for the CIA," Morris adds. "After my service in Naval Intelligence, it was the next logical step for me after the war. Told everyone I was going home to work for my dad, but I took a wrong turn to Langley instead."

I lean back in my chair and let out a deep breath. Morris with the CIA makes a certain kind of sense. I know that back in the Navy, he spent some time with the boys from OSS—the precursor to our current spook agency. He made a lot of contacts in the intelligence community while stationed in the Philippines.

I look over at Angelique and shake my head. I'm just having a really hard time wrapping my head around that one.

"Joe, I'm sorry," she says, offering me an understanding nod. "We don't 'ave time to explain it all to you, at da moment. Like I said, d'ere's trouble a'brewin' on da island, and we need your help."

There's the familiar double tap at the door again, and Clarise appears once more, this time carrying a pot of coffee and three cups with saucers.

"I asked Clarise to prepare us some of d'is 'cause I knew we were gonna need it," Angelique explains, while sitting back and letting the maid pour us each a piping hot cup of Joe. We wait for her to finish and leave the room before continuing.

"What on Earth is going on?" I ask, taking a sip from the cup and wishing I hadn't. The tip of my tongue is now stinging to beat the band. I blow on the steaming liquid before trying again. "I mean, what are you guys mixed up in?"

"Not just us, pal," Morris chimes in. "You're smack dab in this mess, too."

"Me? How?"

My old friend throws me the 'you know what I'm talking about' look I know so well. And it hits me like a bag of bricks dropping on my head.

"The cargo."

He nods, and I turn my attention back to Angelique. "But it was just a standard haul. Untaxed booze and candy for the kids. I saw it when Monday's guy cracked the crate open."

"And do you really t'ink da Governor would go to all d'at trouble just to confiscate one of your typical runs, Joe?" Angelique asks. "Do you t'ink he'd put such a fear in a man like Monday Renot, d'at he would be bold enough to stare me husband down and take da cargo anyway?"

Ah, hell. Why did didn't I think about that sooner?

I take another sip of the coffee to calm my nerves and wipe away a stream of sweat from my brow. It's way too hot in the parlor to be drinking the stuff, but I keep at it anyway. I feel parched. My throat is swelling up from what I can only assume is the gazillion butterflies flapping around in my stomach.

"We need those crates back, Joe," Morris says. "We need them back at all costs, or at least one island in the Caribbean— maybe more, I'm not sure—could be ground zero for a major communist uprising. And soon."

I shake my head. "What the heck was in those crates anyway?"

Morris and Angelique look at each other, then cock their heads in silent debate.

"We can't tell you precisely, Joe," Angelique says. "Da less you know, da better it is for everyone. But inside that crate is a list…"

I try to concentrate on what she's saying, but my world is spinning out of control. A communist uprising? Spies in the Caribbean? My hands clutch the armrests of my chair to steady myself. The room is whirling around me, and I feel like I'm on fire. That coffee is just incredibly hot. My shirt feels as though I've gone for a swim, I'm sweating so much.

"…I was in Cuba a few weeks back." Morris is now talking, but it seems as though he's a million miles away. "I was tracking down a couple of KGB agents, Alexi Krashnov and Vladimir Petrovic—two of the mooks that are here on the island now. They were having clandestine meetings with a few radical upstarts in the region, giving them their own little communist manifesto, if you take my meaning. I was able to get my hands on a guest list right before my cover was blown. But I managed to sneak the list onto some cargo heading out of Havana. My contacts assured me the cargo would be shipped here, to the local SDECE agent, so I hid the list inside one of the crates and got the heck out of Dodge. But it looks like Alexi and Vlad managed to track me down here."

"But...why... What...?"

I'm struggling to formulate a simple sentence, and I'm beginning to wonder if there's more to the coffee I've been drinking than beans and water.

"Now, this list..." Morris just keeps going, oblivious to the room spinning uncontrollably around me. "...I couldn't just fold it up and put it where it could easily be found..." I wish he'd stop talking and let me get a word in edgewise. "...got pretty creative in how I handled it. Used some stuff we learned in the war..." And still he goes on and on, and I'm feeling every bit like death warmed over.

Why aren't they feeling it?

I feel my eye begin to roll back inside my skull. I hear Angelique move from her spot. Feel her presence near me, shaking my shoulders and asking if I'm okay.

I'm not okay. But I'm not quite sure why. Everything feels so heavy around me. My muscles won't move. I try to talk, but my lips won't part.

And then, everything goes black.

CHAPTER 7

Now

"**S**o what happened next?" The man's accent is thick French, which makes sense. Gregor Decroux, the man sitting just outside my jail cell, is the French-appointed regional Detective Inspector of the Guadeloupe Archipelago, stationed on Martinique.

I shake my head, still trying to clear it of the mickey from last night.

"What happened next?" I realize I'm dealing with a real Poindexter here. "I just told you. I passed out. Everything went dark. Then, I wake up handcuffed, with a dear friend dead with a bullet in her head, and the whole island hating me. That's what happened next."

Inspector Decroux strokes at his pencil mustache in thought, then jots something down on his little notebook.

I've pretty much told the Inspector everything I remember about last night—though I've left out a few key details from my narrative. To his knowledge, Morris Grant wasn't even present last night. I haven't even told him I know the guy, actually. And I've completely left out how Angelique was a spy with the SDECE. The detective might be French, but that doesn't mean he's a patriot. For all I know, he's as much of a Red as Alexi and Vlad, the two KGB agents who tracked Morris down to St. Noel.

No, I've got to be careful with how much I reveal, and I've got to try to clear my name while I'm at it.

"And you remember nothing prior to passing out, as you say?"

"Like I said, Angelique and I were just catching up. I haven't seen her in a few weeks. Just two old friends spending time together."

He continues to scribble in his notepad. "Her husband..." He turns back a few pages in the notepad to read the name. "...a Monsieur Jacques Lagrange. He says you were there to have your fortune told?"

I shrug. "That's what Angelique is known for. She'd been giving readings throughout the festival."

"Did you see anyone at ze residence last night to suggest that this was true?" he asks, running the eraser of his pencil along the contours of his Clark Gable mustache.

I think about it for a minute, then shake my head. "Come to think of it, no. When I got there, she was alone in the parlor. Her housekeeper took me to her after the Candyman dropped me off at their bungalow."

I think about it some more. That really is strange. Island-wide celebrations like the St. Noel Festival of the Dead are notorious for Angelique's readings. The place should have been crawling with people waiting for their futures to be revealed. But besides Morris, Clarise, and Angelique, the place was empty.

"So let me ask you," Decroux says. "If it was just you and

Mrs. Lagrange there, how can you expect me to think anything different than that *you* killed her?"

"But I wasn't the only one there. Like I said, Clarise, the maid, was there, too."

"Are you suggesting that she shot her mistress?"

At this point, I'd suggest anything. I know for a fact that I didn't. At least, I *think* I didn't. I can't imagine how I could. Despite her romantic advances toward me, I loved that woman dearly. I love her husband just as much—even though I'm pretty sure he's ready to string me up by my toenails at the moment.

"Look, Inspector." I point to the patch covering my eye. "I'm a pilot. A sailor. I've never been a gunslinger or a marksman. With this bum eye, I'm a lousier shot than when I had two of them. I saw Angelique. Saw the bullet wound dead center in her forehead. There's no way I have accuracy like that."

Decroux nods his head at that, jotting down more notes.

"Good point, but it really means nothing. You were alone with her. You both had been drinking heavily—homemade whisky, if I'm not mistaken." He leans back in the wooden chair he's occupying, and it creaks under his weight. "Maybe she passed out first, eh? Maybe you walked up to her unconscious body and pulled ze trigger at close range?"

I hadn't thought about that possibility. I can't imagine myself ever shooting an unconscious person...especially someone who's no threat to me. But then, I never imagined a day would come where I would be accused of murder either.

If only the inspector could talk to Morris. He'd put everything right. He'd...

That's when it hits me. I struggle to remember the murder scene, as I was dragged out of the parlor by Chief Armad's thugs. Angelique lying lifeless on the floor underneath the table. The red velvet drapes. The tray cart with the pot of coffee on it.

My mind races, trying to get a better mental image of the table. There are two cups of coffee on it. There should have been *three*. The one where I was sitting wasn't there. At least, if my hazy memory is telling me the truth.

But worst of all, there's no trace of my old friend Morris Grant. He's not dead on the floor next to Angelique. He's not walking around the scene with the police officers, and he's not outside in the crowd of gawkers. There's no trace of him anywhere in my memory of this morning. No wonder it's been so easy not to talk about him, when I was telling the Inspector what happened. They genuinely don't know he was even there last night.

So, that begs the question: Where'd he go? Where is he now?

"Monsieur Thacker?" Inspector Decroux brings me back from my whirling thoughts. "Are you listening?"

I look up at him from my cot in the cell. "I'm sorry, what?"

"I asked if you might not have anything else to add in your defense."

"Why bother? Sounds like you already have me convicted anyway."

Decroux offers me a tight smile, then stands from his chair and tucks his small notepad into the pocket of his linen blazer. "I have a few more enquiries to conduct yet, before I make my final conclusion and, of course, I'm going to have to wait until ze ballistics analysis comes back on ze bullet in Mrs. Lagrange's head."

"Small bit of good that'll do," I say. "I was unconscious. Anyone could have used my gun and bullets to kill her."

He shrugs. "Whatever you think of ze French government, Monsieur Thacker, we pride ourselves on having a fair justice system. I assure you, I *will* get to the bottom of this little mystery, whether you believe it or not." He begins walking toward the exit, then turns to look at me. "In ze meantime, I plan on moving you to a Martinique jail, first thing tomorrow morning. Trust me when I say, it's more for your own protection than anything else. After all, you've caused quite a stir on this quiet little island, and I'd hate for mob justice to prevail."

With that, he waves his goodbye and walks out the exit.

The Inspector gone, I lie back on my bunk with my hands under my head for a pillow, and I stare up at the cracked ceiling above me. The cot is little more than a feeding trough filled to the brim with palmetto fronds for a mattress. It's covered in a filthy yellow sheet that I believe used to be white. It feels lumpy under my weight, but I suppose it'll have to do for the time being.

My thoughts are like a tsunami rushing through my mind, trying to put the fractured pieces of my memory together. What happened last night when I blacked out? There were only three other people in the house: Angelique, Morris, and the maid, Clarise.

I sit up.

Clarise.

She's the one who served the coffee. She's the one who had the opportunity to drug it.

I struggle to remember the events more clearly. I drank my entire cup, if I'm not mistaken. But did Morris? Did Angelique? And where did Morris go? He's already a wanted man on the island for suspicion of espionage. I've seen the wanted poster myself. So I can understand him not wanting to hang around for the coppers to show up. But would he leave me to swing by a rope, knowing full well that I didn't kill my friend?

But he and Clarise were getting along splendidly, when I

arrived at the Lagrange bungalow last night. Granted, it's an assumption on my part, but the disheveled appearance of the maid upon my arrival and Morris' showing up a few minutes later in an equal state of disarray speaks volumes. The two were playing footsies when I got there last night. There's no doubt in my mind. So the question is, were they working together?

I hear the door to the cell block creak open and hushed whispers down the hall. I crane my head to see who my latest visitor is, and my blood ices over in my veins.

The Candyman, his face a tight mask of grief and rage, lumbers down the hallway toward my cell. His ham hock-like fists are clenched tight by his sides. He's wearing his customary white linen suit and his wide-brimmed straw hat. His thong sandals make a *phsss-phhhp* sound as he strolls in my direction. When he gets to my cage, he turns and glares at me.

"Look, before you say anything…" I get up from the cot and move closer, my arms outstretched. Pleading.

He puts a sausage-like finger to his full lips, and I go silent.

My heart is thumping in my chest to beat the band. His face is expressionless now. He's in full control of his emotions, which is probably a good thing for me. At the moment. But I can sense the volcanic rage bubbling under the surface.

"I extended a hand of friendship to you, when you first arrived on da island ten years ago." His voice is low. Quiet. Sad. "I welcomed you into my family. Into my home. My wife loves you like a son."

Well…not exactly.

"I do business wit' you. We dine together. Laugh together. You became more of a brother to me than my own kin."

His eyes look down at me and narrow. His brow crinkles in a way that resembles a topographical map of the Himalayas. I want to protest, but I know better than to interrupt. I know he needs to get this out of his system.

"And on such a sacred night...da night in which we celebrate our dead ancestors...you 'ave da audacity to murder my wife in cold blood?" He pauses for a moment, then opens his mouth wide to unleash a primal roar in my direction. "I will kill you, Joe Thacker. Before you leave d'is cell again, I will ensure you a slow and painful death by my hands. By the loa, you will pay for what you 'ave done."

I've been through quite a bit in my thirty-five years. When I was twelve, hiking through the hills of Kentucky, I stumbled on a bear den. Mother bear and her three cubs. Mama wasn't very happy to see me, and it almost cost me my life. Years later, flying over Manila, my plane was shot down. I was captured and spent four months in a Japanese prison camp. Before escaping, I was starved, tortured, and my eye was put out. I've had bounties on my head, and husbands who've wanted to shoot me dead for finding me canoodling with their lady-loves. And in all that time, I've never been more terrified of anything in my entire life as I am of the look my old friend is giving me now.

He means every word, and he has the power and influence to pull it off.

"Jacques, please. Listen to me..."

But he doesn't. Instead, he turns around and heads to the exit. The door squeals again from opening, and he storms out of sight without another word. I'm suddenly alone again and in big trouble.

CHAPTER 8

I'm dead asleep the next time the cell block door opens. I'm startled awake by the noise. I look up at the tiny barred window of my cell, and I see that darkness has descended on the island like an obsidian blanket. Crickets are singing just outside, and a gentle breeze from the ocean flows smoothly into my cell, cooling off the heat from earlier in the day.

I turn my head to see who's coming, but it's so dark in the cell block, it's hard to tell. I can just make out two slight frames. One of them appears to be slightly hunched over. The other one is petite, but strong and shapely.

I sit up, tensing. After what the Candyman told me earlier, I'm not prepared to trust anyone who approaches. You never know when a dagger will strike out at you in the dark, and I want to be ready when that happens.

The two figures materialize in front of my bars, and I smile. It's a doozy of a smile, too, and the weight on my shoulders seems as light as helium. Nessie and Trixie smile back at me. Their eyes betray their concern for me, but they're genuinely happy to see me.

"How you doin', child?" Nessie asks.

I want to gripe like there's no tomorrow. Want to wail at the sky for the injustice of it all. Want to rage against whoever's done the frame-up job on me. But one look into her warm brown eyes takes all my rage away. She looks so maternal in the soft light of the moon coming through my cell window. The last thing I want to do is show just how scared I really am.

"I'm as good as can be expected, I guess." It's the only thing I can think of to say that doesn't make me sound utterly lost and hopeless. "Been better though." I scrounge up strength enough for a wink. "Could use a shave and a long hot bath."

She chuckles, then reaches into my cell, holding a brown paper bag. "I thought you might be hungry. Made you some curry chicken. D'ere's a bottle of rum in d'ere, too, but don't let d'ose greedy coppers know about it."

I take the bag and sit it on my cot before turning my attention to Trixie.

"Hiya, Doll," I say.

"Hi, yourself." She's having trouble looking me in the eye. "We would have come to visit sooner, but I had a show tonight. Had to wait until it was over."

I nod. "Completely understand. Don't want a riot in the streets when Trixie Faye fails to make an appearance."

She laughs. It's a quiet, sad laugh, and I want nothing more than to take her in my arms and comfort her.

"I need you two to know something," I say, before the encounter can get any more awkward. "I didn't do it. I didn't kill Angelique."

They both look at me, and their eyes shine in the dim light. "We know," Trixie says.

That throws me for a loop. "You know?"

69

She nods. "I overheard the Russians this morning, talking about the whole thing."

"They admitted to framing me?"

"Not exactly." She blinks as if trying to remember. "They were talking about Angelique…and some American that's been hiding on the island."

Morris.

"It was crazy talk, really," she continues. "Stuff about how Angelique was a spy, and how between the two of them, they had some important information—a list or something—that they needed to get their hands on. They said that you were somehow involved in it all, too."

"Me? Why do they think I'm involved?" Although I'm certain I can trust these two with the entirety of last night's conversation, I think it best to play dumb for the moment. For their own protection more than anything else.

"They said you and the American are old friends," Trixie answers. "Said the three of you were meeting in Angelique's parlor last night when she was killed."

I say nothing for a moment, rubbing the stubble growing across my chin, as I process. I already suspected the Reds had something to do with my current predicament. I even shared my theory with Inspector Decroux. But with the protections they're enjoying from Governor Lagrange, I'm pretty sure the Inspector won't get very far digging into the Reds' stories.

Then, there's the list itself. Uncle Sam needs to get a hold of it before the Ruskies do. I have no doubt it's vital to national security, and while I've been living it up in paradise for the past decade, I'm first and foremost an American. I bleed red, white, and blue. And even though I'm currently fighting for my life with a murder rap, I've spent most of my adult life defending my country. It's ingrained in me. No matter what happens to me, I've got to get that list before the KGB mooks do.

Besides, find the list and I might kill two birds with one stone. I might find evidence that will exonerate me.

I look at my two visitors, then glance around, making sure no one else is within earshot. "Okay, ladies," I say. "I've got to get out of here. Tonight. And I'm going to need your help to do it."

The two of them smile and lean forward. They're all ears, as I pitch my escape plan to them in a hushed voice.

CHAPTER 9

3:00 AM

I've just started to doze off when the sound of scratching at my barred window shakes the sleep away with a jolt. I open my eye to see Moe's fur-covered face grinning down at me, a set of keys tied around his neck.

So Trixie managed to pull it off, I think, standing on top of the bunk and letting the monkey leap down onto my shoulders. I'm not really surprised. There's not a man on the island who doesn't yearn to get close to her. It would be a relatively simple thing for her to lift the cell keys, as she put on the flirtation act with one of the two coppers tasked with posting guard in the station. Step one, give him the goo-goo eyes. Step two, give a little tickle underneath his chin with one hand. Step three, lift the key-ring from his belt while he whispers sweet nothings in her ear. Piece of cake.

Of course, the real challenge will be to sneak out of here, before the officer discovers his keys are missing. And unfortunately, there's no way to guess when that will…

Someone starts banging a metal gong from somewhere in the police station. "Escape!" someone shouts. "Escape!"

"Well, crap," I mutter, while unlocking my cell door with the keys and moving toward the block door. I'm not exactly sure how the discovery of missing keys necessitates cries of escape to arouse the citizens of the island into action. Seems to me, whichever officer is currently on duty would have come into the block to check on me first, before assuming the worst.

Unless…

But how could he have been tipped off? Only Nessie and Trixie know about my plans.

It doesn't matter for now. With the alarm being raised, I'm out of time. If I'm going to escape, clear my name, and retrieve the list, I need to get out of here undetected. And fast.

I prepare to insert the key into the cell block door and hesitate.

Or maybe, fast isn't the answer this time.

I allow a smile to creep up the side of my face. What I'm thinking is risky. Very risky. But I also know that Chief Armad and his men will be on high alert for the rest of the night. I need to be smart, not swift in my escape.

Taking a breath, I unlock the cell block door and open it. I can hear shouts from the squad room in front of the police station, then feet pounding the linoleum floors heading my way. Without waiting another heartbeat, I nudge Moe off my shoulder and watch him leap to the bars of my cell, just before I dash off to set my escape plan in motion.

———

"I DON'T UNDERSTAND! How, pray tell, could Thacker get a key to the cells?" Chief Armad is giving Lloyd Gano, the youngest officer on the force, a verbal lashing he won't forget. I guess he was the one on guard duty during my escape.

Moe is still in my cell, swinging from bar to bar in cheerful play.

"I...I don't 'ave any idea, Chief," Lloyd protests. "I had d'em when I came on duty tonight."

Armad turns to the monkey. His eyes narrow into slits, as he draws his revolver from its holster and takes aim. He fires, but Moe's been around guns long enough. He's smart enough to get out of the way, when they're pointed in his direction. Before the gun's explosion finishes echoing around the room, the monkey leaps from the bars to the window and makes good his escape.

With a deeply unsatisfied look on his face, the Chief steps into my cell and sighs. He examines the lock mechanism of the door, then his gaze moves up to the barred window, then to the ceiling.

He sighs and turns to Marvin and Lloyd with a huff.

"He can't have gotten far," Armad says. "Besides, the entire island is out to get him. No one's going to help him hide from us for long." He comes within an inch of Lloyd's nervous face. "We'll discuss just how you let the man escape later. For now, we've got to search the town."

His two officers stand there, looking at him like beaten mongrels.

"Let's go! Let's go!" he shouts, clapping his hands together to get them moving. Without comment, the three men bolt from the cell block, leaving me perfectly hidden in the hiding spot I chose for myself earlier.

I'M NOT sure how long I wait. It's deep into the night now. My cell is dark, and the moonlight that was passing through the barred window has slipped from sight. I'm hiding amid the palm fronds of my bunk and peering through the tiniest of tears in the bed sheets. I've waited patiently, listening to the sounds of angry voices far outside my window, hurling accusations at Armad and his 'incompetent' police force over my escape from their jail. I heard the same voices scatter, scouring the narrow alleyways between the town's buildings and heading into the jungle. I'm certain that quite a few of them have already headed toward Port Lucine's pier to search the *Dream*. I shudder to think what the angry mob might do to her to deal with their frustrations over my escape.

I wait just a bit longer, then I begin to dig my way out of my hiding place. The voices have all but gone now, but I can't begin to guess how long they'll remain out of earshot. The whole of my plan depends on setting everyone's eyes somewhere else, after all. It'll do me no good to wait too long only to have them return as I'm sneaking out the door. Come to think of it, I've already pushed my luck to no end with the pile of palm fronds I tossed out my window while digging away at my hiding space. It's a miracle no one has stumbled across it yet.

I give a soft whistle, and Moe's head peers through the window bars again. He scrambles into my cell, scurries up my leg, and onto my back.

"Glad to see the Chief is a lousy shot," I say to him, giving the wall to my cell a once-over and seeing the hole where his bullet struck. Not only did he miss the monkey, he also missed the bunk in which I was hiding by about twelve inches. Appraising just how lucky I am that I'm not currently a rotting corpse inside a feeding trough, I turn to the cell block door again, which is still ajar. I move over to the door and listen.

There doesn't seem to be anyone about, so I scramble out into the hallway, weave my way through to the back of the station, and quickly find myself at the back exit.

Cautiously, I crack open the door and let Moe step into the night. He scrambles a few feet away, looks around, then sits down on his haunches to start picking at mites under his arms. It's his own unique way, I suppose, of telling me the coast is clear.

Putting my life in the fleabag's hands, I duck outside, scoop him up in my arms, and sprint into the nearest stand of trees.

The jungle is abuzz with the lights of lanterns and flashlights slicing away at the darkness, as the mob stomps through the undergrowth beating the bushes for me. I hear the bray of hounds—thankfully somewhere far in the distance. I know that whatever I do and wherever I go, I'll need to keep as much distance from the dogs as I possibly can. I hear shouts to my left, and cries asking others to join them when they think they see something suspicious.

I move into the jungle interior for about a hundred yards, then stop, crouching behind a palmetto bush and taking a deep breath. Moe's already taken to the trees. I like to think he's keeping a bird's eye view of the hunt, but in reality, I'm pretty sure he's just looking for a snack to eat.

Stupid monkey.

I look up into the sky, peering past the canopy of vegetation. The stars above are starting to fade. Although I don't have a clear view of the eastern horizon, I can picture it in my mind's eye turning shades of purple, lavender, and orange-red in thin ribbons, just where land and ocean touch the sky. The sun will be coming up soon, which means I need to find shelter as quick as possible. Daylight will be my undoing, if I'm left exposed in it for too long.

Keeping low to the ground, I press on, avoiding the

dangers of dried palm fronds, broken twigs, and anything else that might echo my location to anyone near enough to hear. I weave in and out of the trees, trying to keep as many obstructions between myself and the posse that's now hunting me.

Despite my attempts at stealth, however, it's been a long time since my days as an Eagle Scout. With legs and feet more suited to sea or air, and with the depth perception of a man with a single eye, I'm not quite as skilled an Indian tracker as I would like. In the dim light, my boot comes down on something jutting up from the wet soil. I stumble forward, crashing to the ground with a thud and a hiss of air from my lungs. The resulting noise echoes through the rainforest like an audible neon sign flashing 'OVER HERE!'

Worse, someone hears it.

I freeze.

The hunters near me do the same. I hear hushed whispers nearby.

I crane my head around, trying to spot where the voices are coming from, but the jungle creates just as much of a blind for me as it does for them.

A jungle, after all, is impartial in both its cruelty and its loving embrace. There are no good guys or bad guys in the jungle. There is only the game of survival, and the jungle revels in the contest between the strongest wills.

Suddenly, I hear the shout.

"Over here!" someone cries. "He's over here!"

All I can do in response is run.

CHAPTER 10

My feet nearly fly out from under me as I sprint through the thick vegetation, almost fall over, balance myself, and continue to run. The mob is behind me, shouting obscenities and curses at me as they pursue. From my periphery, I can see that Moe is keeping pace with me, leaping from tree limb to branch with little effort. He's chattering away, egging me on. My one and only cheerleader.

His cheers are appreciated. I press on, ignoring the slicing lashes of the palmetto fronds as they whip past my face. My lungs heave for air, and I find myself cursing at my cigar-smoking habit within the first mile of the run. My only saving grace is that over half the population of the island—including the island police—have the same, or worse habits than I do.

The good news is that the hounds I heard earlier don't seem to be among the mix of my pursuers. I'm not sure whether it's because they were so far away when I was first spotted or something else, but at least I don't have fanged jaws snapping at my heels as I flee.

The bad news is, if my memory of this part of the jungle is

accurate, I'm running out land. I'm not exactly sure where it is, but I know there's a deep gorge somewhere up ahead. There's a rope bridge somewhere as well, but once again, I can't be certain I'm on the right course to meet up with it. After all, I'm not on an actual path, and this area isn't exactly sketched out on any map.

The shouts behind me are getting louder. Angrier.

I risk a quick glance over my shoulder. Around eight men —all carrying lanterns, as well as farm hoes, pitchforks, and other makeshift weapons made from farming tools—are right behind me. I see no sign of Armad and his police officers, nor the Candyman, and I thank my lucky stars for that blessing. Then again, almost every person on the island practices voodoo, and they all think I've killed their mamba. None of them are going to listen to reason or pleas to give me a chance.

But I don't have time to think about that now. The jungle is thinning just ahead of me—the telltale sign of the approaching gorge. The sheer cliff face and the drop that will turn my bones to powder, if I'm not careful.

The only good news at the moment is the rising sun. Although it's still below the horizon of the jungle, its waxing light is already beginning to cut through the gloom, allowing me to see where I'm going a lot better. Unfortunately, it also lets my pursuers see me much better, making it nearly impossible to shake them off my tail. To escape, I'm going to have to do something stupid.

Something radical.

Something that'll probably get me killed.

As the gorge's drop-off creeps into view, I search for anything that might give me an idea, and my mind races through everything I know about the terrain ahead. I know the gorge is about a forty-five foot drop. Depending on the tide, not to mention the weather, the river that cuts through the island to create the gorge increases and decreases in depth. Once again, there's a bridge that's been constructed to safely cross it, but I have no way of knowing where it is, in relation to my position in the jungle.

My brain falters. My feet hesitate. The slightest miscalculation...the smallest slip-up...and I'm dead.

Something slams into the back of my head. A stone.

Those mooks are throwing rocks at me now.

Another stone whacks my shoulder.

"Stop throwing rocks at me!" I shout, leaping over a dead tree and pushing my legs beyond their limits.

And then, I'm forced to stop. Fast. I've run out of ground. The deadly drop is only a few feet in front of me. Despite my brain screaming at my feet to halt, it still takes a couple of seconds to register. Finally, they listen, and I hit the brakes, lean back, and slide across the jungle floor. My fingers scratch at the soil, grass, and vines, desperately searching for anything that'll save me from going over the edge.

When I finally do come to a halt, my feet are dangling over the cliff, and my right hand is clutching a tiny sapling. It's nearly pulled out by its roots, but it's doing its job by keeping me on solid ground. Mostly.

I lower my face in the dirt and exhale.

"Jeepers, that was a close one," I mumble. My mouth is now full of dirt, as I let out a nervous laugh. I raise my head to spit it from my mouth and stare into the faces of eight angry men. The business ends of their pitchforks and hoes are pointing at me, and each of their eyes are angry slits looking in my direction.

I give them a friendly smile, irrationally hoping it'll make all this go away. But Mama Thacker's boy never had very good luck, and I don't see why it should change now. Truth is, I know these men. Good men, each of them. I've shared drinks with them at Nessie's or at the Candyman's. Played poker with most of them. Helped repair their homes after hurricanes. They're a part of my community, and I'm a part of theirs.

"Hiya, fellas," I say, slowly—and carefully—climbing to my feet. I make sure to keep my hands in the air, once my feet are solidly on *terra firma*.

One of the men, the town barber, Winston Musel, shakes his head at me. Unlike his friends, his eyes are more sad than angry. "How could you, Joe? I just don't understand."

"Join the club. I don't either." I stretch out my hands, pleading for them to listen. "Look, fellas, I don't know what happened. Someone drugged me. When I came to, Angelique was dead. But I know I didn't kill her. There's no way I would have done something like that." I level my gaze at them, looking at each one of them, and looking them square in the eyes. "You know that. I'm no killer. And even if I was, I loved Angelique just as much as any of you here."

They stare at me, and for the first time, I see doubt in their eyes. And, just as the sun begins to shine its first light of the day through the eastern edge of jungle, hope begins to rise within my chest. They look at each other, offering confused expressions.

"It certainly don't sound like somet'ing you would do," Winston says. His steel rake lowers a few inches. The other weapons do the same.

My heart thumps madly in my chest. I'm getting through to them.

I'm just about to continue my logical defense when the unthinkable happens. A loud bang explodes off to my left. The jungle fills with light gray smoke tinged with the smell of sulfur. Then a crimson circle begins to spread across the shirt covering Winston's belly. His eyes go wide. He grits his teeth and begins to tumble backward. Tomas Musel, Winston's brother, dashes to him, catching him before he hits the ground.

"No!" I shout, spinning around and searching for the gunman who shot the barber. For a brief second, I catch the slightest trace of a brightly colored, flower-print shirt darting from one tree to the next.

Morris?

"Don't hurt them!" I yell at my old friend. "Stand down!"

The others see him, too, and they begin pointing in his direction with angry shouts. But their attacker has a gun. They don't. With betrayal in their eyes as they look at me, Tomas and another man lift Winston up, and the eight men begin running back to town to seek medical treatment.

"I had nothing to do with that!" I yell at them as they flee, but if they hear me, they don't respond.

Now angry at my friend, I wheel around to search for him, prepared to give him a piece of my mind. Although I appreciate him coming to my rescue during my escape, I am beyond angry over how he chose to do it.

Those men were no threat to me. They were listening to what I had to say. Believing me. And Morris couldn't have been far enough away that he couldn't have heard them. So why'd he do it? Why take the cheap shot like that?

"Morris?" I shout. "They're gone. You can come out now!"

He doesn't respond, and there's no movement anywhere near me.

"Morris?"

I wait five heartbeats and glance up in a nearby tree. Moe is staring down at me, gnawing on a nut of some kind.

"Did you see where he went?" I let out a low growl of frustration. "Of course not. That would make you useful for a change."

Satisfied the excitement is over and with his fill of foraged nuts, the monkey clambers down the tree and leaps onto my back once more. I give the top of his head a pat, while scanning the area for a ridiculously bright red shirt. But there's no sign at all.

Swell. Leave me high and dry at Angelique's. Shoot an innocent man in the gut. Then disappear all over again.

"Who's side are you on anyway?" I shout into the jungle.

I freeze at the thought. I had meant it as a joke, but the more I consider it, the more the question makes a lot of sense. Just whose side *is* Morris Grant on? He's a spy, sure. But whose spy? Does he really work for the Central Intelligence Agency, like he claims? Sure, I've been buddies with the guy for years, but I don't really know much about him. Not really.

An ice cold wave of dread washes up my spine.

Did Morris kill Angelique and frame me for it?

The sound of braying rips me away from my runaway thoughts. The posse is back on the trail. Our little run put me at a pretty good distance from town. Winston and his men can't have possibly made it back there yet to inform everyone where I am. But the dogs are a reminder that I'm not out of the...well, out of the woods yet.

"First things first," I say to Moe in a whisper. "We need to find a good place to lay low for the time being. Then, we can figure out what Morris is up to."

With that, I turn south and begin following the edge of the cliff as quietly, but as quickly as I can, searching for the rope bridge that will lead me deeper into uncharted jungle. And hopefully, to freedom.

CHAPTER 11

The sun now hangs directly above me, heating the jungle up like an unattended pressure cooker. Every breath I take feels like I'm swallowing a wet sponge. Sweat pours down my face, burns into my eye, and works to cool down my neck and back, as I trudge forward into sections of the island I've never traveled before.

Geographically, St. Noel is a rather small island, stretching roughly thirteen miles north to southwest in an apostrophe-shaped volcanic landmass. Although there are a few fishing and farming colonies along the coastline, as well as a large sugar cane plantation owned by none other than Governor Lagrange, the island only has one permanent settlement: Port Lucine, with a population of maybe one hundred and fifty people. The town is a tightly packed, close-knit community. The remaining eighty-seven percent of the island is mostly untamed wilderness that's proved far more difficult to develop than it's worth. And while there are no large land predators or venomous snakes to contend with, the few dangers that *are* present in the jungle are enough to discourage many islanders from venturing into the interior to explore. The only ones I know of who brave the unmapped wilderness are a handful of miners looking for veins of bauxite, which is plentiful on St. Noel, and some of the more courageous kids who come out to hunt for whistling frogs that they catch for pets.

For the most part, the island's interior is like being marooned on a desert island, and that's what I'm counting on. While small, St. Noel's lush landscape and rugged terrain provides me with the best possible coverage to avoid the posse I have no doubt is still hunting me down.

At the same time, wherever I decide to set up shop, it can't be too far away from Port Lucine. I can't live out here forever. I need to be able to come and go into town easily enough to investigate who killed Angelique and framed me. And to find the blasted list the KGB lugs are so hot and bothered over. Which means, now that I'm good and royally lost, I need to turn around and find a good spot for a base camp. It has to be far enough away from town to keep me safe, while close enough to allow me quick and easy access to anything I might need.

An hour later, I'm drenched from head to toe with sweat, but now it's an easy five mile hike to town. Far enough out of the way to keep prying eyes from seeing me. So, I spend the next thirty minutes or so looking for a place to call 'home.' A cave, perhaps. Or at least an outcrop of rocks along the nearby range of hills that can hide a campfire.

What I find instead is far more ghastly. As I walk quietly through the palms and banana trees that cover the ground like the hairs on the head of an immense giant, I notice something horrid and foul in the air. A distinct, unmistakable scent of decay.

I sniff, trying to pinpoint the location of the putrefaction, and I move farther south. Soon, I begin to hear a low, gentle hum in a clearing about a hundred yards in front of me. As I approach, the humming grows louder, until I reassess the sound as more of a buzzing.

I quickly locate the source of the noise, as I enter the clearing.

The entire area is covered in blood, soaking into the ground. A vast cloud of flies buzz through the air, landing here and there, wherever the faintest traces of blood and viscera might be found.

I can't help but stifle a gag, as I take in the sight and smell of the place, but I focus my mind on deciphering what transpired here.

An iron cauldron sits, cold and lifeless, on the remains of what used to be a fire pit. Though the firewood is now cold, the ash still smolders, and a slight trace of smoke still spirals into the sky. I peer into the cauldron. Sticks of various sizes and lengths protrude from the opening. Everything else inside appears as little more than char and ash.

I've seen similar sights before. Nearby islands have practitioners of a religion known as Palo Mayombe, a much darker, scarier faith than voodoo could ever be. Those who practice Palo use similar cauldrons, known as *ngangas*, which are used for all manner of dreadful rituals.

Carefully, I take one of the sticks from the cauldron and start stirring the contents, hoping to disprove my theory. But I'm disappointed when the churning stick slowly uncovers the charred remains of a human skull, a handful of ribs, and a long bone. It's precisely what I thought it was. A ritual *nganga*, recently utilized in a ceremony, no doubt, to curse someone. Considering I'm the island's current *numero uno* on the Most Wanted list, I'm pretty sure it wouldn't take me more than one guess to identify the curse's intended target.

Or the one who placed the curse to begin with.

The Candyman.

But Jacques Lagrange doesn't practice Palo Mayombe. He's a voodoo priest. He's always found the other religion's obsession with death and revenge to be distasteful. A disgrace to the loa, who he serves. If the Candyman has taken to the dark religion, now that his wife was so callously murdered, it means he's become truly unhinged. There's no telling what he'll do to me, if he actually gets his hands around my neck.

I swat away a circling fly, as I study the ritualistic scene. Several headless chickens have been strewn around the clearing, their blood no doubt used to fuel the magic Jacques intended to summon. Weird symbols and glyphs, painted in the same blood, are scrawled along the trees around me. I'm not sure whether the site is a warning to me, or if I was even supposed to see the place, but I can't control the shiver that vibrates down my body as I take it all in.

But one thing is abundantly clear to me now. First, I'll have to be even more cautious from this point forward than I originally planned. Better to spend the rest of my life in a French prison than to let the Candyman get ahold of me. Second, the site is a painful reminder that I'm far too close to Port Lucine to make a safe camp. I'll need to move on and find a better spot, because I have no idea whether Jacques and his followers will return to conduct even more secret dark magic against me. And if they do, I better not be within three miles of this place.

I'm about to press on when something crunches in the woods behind me. I turn around, reaching for the gun in my shoulder holster, only to remember it was confiscated when I was arrested yesterday morning. With no weapon to defend myself, I dash across the blood-soaked earth and move behind a tree, waiting and watching for whatever made the sound.

There's another crunch, the sound of a foot coming down on the detritus of fallen branches littering the jungle floor. I crouch down, preparing myself to pound on anyone who enters the sacrificial clearing. Every muscle in my body tenses, despite my exhaustion from the escape from the jail.

More footsteps echo slightly off to my left, maybe less than a few dozen yards away. Whoever it is doesn't seem concerned with stealth.

My hands are clenched into tightly wound fists now.

I rock back and forth on the balls of my feet, still crouched and well out of sight from anyone not directly behind me.

I see movement: a pair of bare brown legs and old worn sneakers. I blink and do a double-take. The legs are small, attached to someone wearing a pair of ragged shorts and a baseball mitt on one hand. He stops when he sees the carnage in the clearing, his little eyes stretch twice their normal size, as his mouth drops open.

"Malik?" I say, standing from my hiding spot.

The young orphan boy jumps at the sound of my voice. He turns to me, and a smile instantly spreads across his face.

"Cap'n Joe! I found you!"

He turns his attention back to the sacrificial site, and his smile melts away with worry.

"Malik, don't look at it," I say. "Keep your eyes on me. Just keep them on me."

The boy is an islander, born and raised. Although Nessie has tried to raise him Catholic, I know he's been to a great number of the voodoo ceremonies that happen on St. Noel all the time...ceremonies involving sacrifices and blood. He's used to it. But seeing his nervous demeanor around the grue-some sight in the clearing makes me feel better that I haven't exaggerated its significance. There's something about the bloody tableau that's just wrong. Evil. And Malik doesn't seem to like it any more than I do.

The boy, keeping his eyes locked on mine, circumvents the clearing and runs to me. I watch him as he struggles not to let his eyes drift back to the gruesome vision, but he finally makes it to me and wraps his arms around my waist in a big hug.

I crouch down, take his shoulders in my hands, and look at him. "Malik, what are you doing out here? You shouldn't be here."

Secretly, I'm on cloud nine at seeing such a friendly face. If he knows what's going on—what I've been accused of—he doesn't seem to believe it. He's trusting me, literally, with open arms, and that means the world to me.

"I 'ad to come," he says. "Miss Trixie asked me to find you. Told me everyt'ing. Told me you were innocent and d'at you needed my help."

Bless that woman.

Then, reality hits. "Malik, you can't help me. If you get caught helping me, you'll be accused..."

"They won't catch us, Cap'n Joe. Never." His bright smile is infectious. "I know d'is jungle better d'an anybody. I take you someplace no one will ever find you."

"Really? Where?"

He takes off to the east, waving at me to follow. With no reason to argue, I run after him and hope to God I'm not leading the kid down a rotten path.

CHAPTER 12

We can't have walked more than a mile or two before Malik begins to slow down. He turns his head to look at me as he comes to a full stop. "We're here."

I look around, but all I see are the same hills, trees, bushes, and web-like vines I've been seeing all day. Before I can protest, he hands me his mitt and waits for me to reverently tuck it under my arm before he turns again to face the wall of ivy directly in front of him. He reaches out and begins pulling the vines apart, until he reveals the opening of a low-ceilinged cave and points.

Moe takes a look at the cave entrance and lets out a series of nervous whoops.

"Oh, stop being such a wise guy," I say to the monkey. "It's not so bad."

"Yes, Moe," Malik laughs. "You'll love it in there. I promise." With that, the kid ducks and slips into the opening without another word.

With a quick look over my shoulders, I crouch and follow, with Moe nearly strangling my neck all the way. I'm just under the lip of the cave when I'm instantly greeted by the warm orange light of torches lining the walls and a campfire just out of sight. I push forward and the cave begins to expand, until I'm standing at full height again. I look up, but the cavern ceiling is beyond my ability to see. This place is, quite simply, huge. And as I look around, I begin to suspect it carries other secrets with it as well.

Along the rock walls to both my left and right, there are a number of large wooden barrels stacked up on top of each other. The type of barrels people store rum in, in fact.

I look over at Malik, who's grinning ear to ear. "It's an old smuggler's hideaway my grandpa told me about before he died," he says. "Back during da time of slavery, grandpa's pa and his pals made rum. D'ey used d'is cavern, and others like it, to store d'eir wares 'til it was time to smuggle d'em off da island."

We walk past the barrels, approaching a bottleneck passage. The campfire light can now be seen clearly on the other side. Malik, for his part, simply walks through with little effort. Moe jumps down and quickly follows the boy. I, on the other hand, am forced to turn sideways and scrape through the passage, while sucking in my breath. It's a tight squeeze, and claustrophobia begins to beat down on me just as I pull through into a vast chamber that stretches far beyond the reach of the firelight.

As we approach the campfire, I see a couple of bedrolls sitting there, as well as an overstuffed backpack. The kid has come prepared, and I pat him on the shoulder to let him know how proud of him I am.

Malik, nodding gratitude for my silent compliment, gestures for me to sit down before taking the mitt from me and setting it down next to his pack. "Miss Trixie told me we now need to wait a while," he says, while rifling through the pack.

A moment later, he withdraws a couple of cigars, a pocket knife, and a pearl-handled Colt .45, and he brings them all over to me before returning to the pack.

The .45 isn't mine, but it'll do real nice in a pinch.

"Where'd you get a gun?" I ask, taking it and slipping it into my holster. I slip the knife in my pants pocket, bite off the tip of a cigar, and use the campfire to light it. Before I've inhaled the first sweet taste of the cigar, Malik pulls out an iron coffee pot, and he walks a few feet outside of my field of vision. Moe is right on his heels, as if the little monkey is his guardian angel or something.

"Nessie wanted you to 'ave it," the kid says in the darkness. "She says you might need it before d'is is all over."

I take another puff of the cigar, silently thanking the old woman for the gift. Then, something Malik said a few minutes ago, leaps to the forefront of my thought.

"Hold on a second," I ask. "What are we supposed to be waiting for?"

Somewhere nearby I hear the gentle trickle of water and the kerplunk of the pot going into some kind of pool. A moment later, Malik appears with a full pot and sets it down on the open flames. The monkey is now clinging to his neck.

"Huh?"

"You said Trixie mentioned that we might have to wait a while. Wait for what?"

The kid looks down at his shoes for a brief second, then, as if he hasn't heard me, he thumbs over his shoulder. "D'ere's an underground river," he says, as he rummages through his pack for two metal cups. "Leads out to da ocean on da other side of da island. It's how my great-grandpa and his pals got da rum off da island wit'out d'eir masters knowin'."

I shake my head, releasing a series of smoke rings in the air to calm my nerves. "That's not what I asked, Malik. Why does Trixie want me to wait here? What's she up to?"

The boy just shrugs. "Don't know. She just told me to keep you here until she arrived."

"She's coming here?" I stand up. "That's just stupid. Crazy broad's gonna get us both caught."

Malik laughs.

"What?" I glare at him.

"Miss Trixie told me you'd say all d'at. Almost word for word."

I roll my eye at the kid, which only makes him giggle some more. I then sit down again, Indian style, and take the cup of coffee he pours me.

"So, what's it like in town now?" I toss the remainder of the cigar into the fire and take a sip of the dark brown liquid. It's passable enough for coffee, but only barely. It's not the kid's fault. Just the product of trying to brew it in such a dank place over open flames.

"It's, how do you always say it? Looney Tunes." He sits across the campfire from me, digs into his pockets, and pulls out three of pieces of candy. He unwraps one and hands it to Moe, who dashes off to the side to munch down on the sweet little treat. Malik then tosses me one and unwraps the other before tossing it into his mouth. "Everyone's so angry. Don't no one believe you're innocent neither. No one 'cept Nessie and Trixie, d'at is."

"And you, apparently." I wink at him, while placing the hard candy in the pocket of my flight jacket.

"Oh, I know you could never kill Mrs. Angelique, Cap'n Joe. You couldn't kill anyone who wasn't a Jap or a Nazi."

I cringe at his words. While it's true that I shot down my share of Japanese pilots in my day, they were kill-or-be-killed situations. It never made me happy to do it, but it sure made me happy to survive any dog fight I happened to find myself in. As for the Nazis, my entire time in the war was spent in the South Pacific. I never faced off against a Jerry, but I don't think I would have been bothered too much to put a few of them down, if I had had the chance. And I'm starting to feel the same about the Reds, too—maybe even more so, now that I'm in the situation I'm in.

All in all, though, I don't like the idea of the kid thinking killing anyone is easy for me. Heck, I came all the way to the Caribbean for peace and quiet...to get away from all the violence and killing of my past.

Still, I'm thankful the boy believes in me.

We sit in silence for a while longer, me enjoying the steaming cup of joe-like beverage and Malik sucking on the hard candy. When my cup is empty, I unfurl the bed roll and lie down on it.

"We should get some rest. I haven't slept—without being drugged anyway—for a couple of days." I lie back on the mat and place my hands behind my head. "I'm exhausted."

"Roger Wilco," Malik says. The boy always loves using radio call phrases whenever he can—even if he gets the context wrong from time to time. He's picked up a few expressions from war pictures he's seen here and there. The rest, unfortunately, he's learned from me, during my frequent story times with him and his friends.

Once he's down, Moe curls up against me on the bedroll, and I stare up at the darkness in thought.

"Hey, Malik?"

"Yeah?"

"I'm curious. Have you seen a fella around lately who wears nutty tropical shirts all the time? Real clean-cut looking. White..."

"You mean, Mrs. Angelique's friend?"

I sit up at that.

"Angelique's friend?" I ask, not sure I've heard him right.

"Sure. I seen him going over to see her a few times, while you were in Cuba. Always sneaking in at night t'rough da back door. He's always careful when he does it, like he's hidin' or somet'ing, but you know…"

The kid's 'you know' refers to the fact that, despite Nessie's part in taking him in and raising him, he's still very much a street urchin. Not much passes along the narrow alleys and dirt walking paths that Malik doesn't see or know about. It's one of the reasons I asked him about Morris to begin with.

"How often did you see him going over there?"

He's quiet for a moment, as if thinking. "Oh, maybe five or six times."

"Did you see him there the night of the festival? The night Angelique was killed?"

"Oh, no. I ain't seen him since a few nights before you got back." It was disappointing news. As much as I would hate to spill the beans on my old pal's presence at the house that night, an eyewitness who said there was someone else in the house at the time of Angelique's murder would go a long way toward exonerating me. At the very least, it would give that French Inspector another possible suspect to look at. "He ain't been back since da Candyman caught him in da house and nearly killed him," Malik continued.

That's news to me.

"Wait, what? Jacques caught him in their house? He knows about him?"

The boy nods at me. "Well, it's not like da Candyman didn't know 'bout da other times. He's the one who let him in da backdoor a couple of da times da man showed up."

Holy smokes. Jacques Lagrange knows Morris, which means, he more than likely knows he's a spy. My heart leaps up into my throat. *So does that mean he knows about Angelique?*

"Wouldn't he have to know?" I mumble to myself.

"What did you say, Cap'n Joe?"

I shake my head. "Nothing, Malik. Just talking out loud."

I lean back on the bedroll again, letting all this new information process.

"Cap'n Joe?"

"Yeah, Malik?"

"If it's okay with you, I t'ink I'll go to sleep now."

I give Moe a good scratch behind the ear, as he nuzzles even closer to me. "Yeah, me too, kid. Me too."

But I know as I utter the words, sleep will be a long time coming, as I ponder everything I've just learned.

CHAPTER 13

I wake to the sound of a small motor boat puttering in our direction. I jump from my bedding and turn toward the subterranean river, but I can't see a blasted thing through the black void beyond the fire's light. Realizing I'm a sitting duck, I scoop up Malik's sleeping form and dash over into the darkness. The boy is startled awake and opens his mouth to shout, but I manage to clamp a hand over his face to silence him.

"Shhhhh," I hiss. "Someone's coming."

Malik struggles in my arms, mumbling something under the palm of my hand, but I don't let up the pressure. Last thing I need is for him to give our position away.

The motorboat—it sounds like a small trolling engine, if I'm not mistaken—putters up to the shore. The engine shuts down, and I hear the little boat's wake slapping against the stone shore, before a pair of feet splash into the water.

Crouching down, with the boy resting on my knees, I pull my gun with my free hand and take aim.

"Mmmbbmmmbbbbbmmm," Malik growls into my hand.

"Would you be quiet?" I whisper.

That's when I realize I've left Moe in camp. He's sitting up on my bedroll, looking around the cavern in a sleepy state of confusion. I want desperately to coax him over to us, but I can't do that without letting the newcomers know we're here.

The monkey picks something from his fur and stuffs it in his mouth, then turns his head toward the water and sniffs. Before I can do anything about it, he bolts off in the direction of the boat with a series of ecstatic whoops.

Stupid monkey's never met a stranger, and it's his unwavering trust that's going to be the death of him one of these days.

I hold my breath, keeping my gun trained at the darkness ahead and my finger firmly on the trigger. I wasn't lying to Inspector Decroux. I'm a terrible shot. But what I've lost in depth perception, a good supply of bullets can easily make up for. And this Colt .45 holds at least seven rounds. Plenty for my needs, as long as there aren't too many people to deal with.

Then, she steps into the firelight.

Moe's tail is wrapped around her delicate and supple porcelain neck. Golden blonde hair is tied in a pony tail behind her head. She's wearing a pair of riding jodhpurs, knee-high leather riding boots, and a man's button-up shirt. An M1 army rifle hangs off her shoulder by a strap. And her coy, closed-mouth smile almost melts my feet to the floor of the cave, as she moves clearly into view.

"You can come out now," Trixie says, with a mocking trace of humor in her voice. "It's just little ol' me, big boy."

I exhale, and every muscle in my body relaxes.

"Trixie?"

Malik pats my arm, reminding me that I've still got him gagged with my hand. I release him and he turns to me. "I was tryin' to tell you. Trixie told me she'd be coming to see us, by way of da river."

We walk over to the camp, and Trixie immediately takes me in her arms and plants a big one right on my kisser.

"Oh, Joe, I'm so glad you're alright," she says afterward. "I've been worried sick."

"Thanks, Doll. But you really shouldn't be here. I don't want you any more involved in this mess than you already are. It was bad enough I asked you to steal the jail key from Lloyd." I gesture toward Malik and the cave. "This is too much. It's making it easier for them to discover you're helping me."

"I don't care if they find out," she says. "You're being rail-roaded, and anyone with half a brain can see that. So, right now, we need to do everything we can to clear your name and find out who's done this frame job on you." She points a lovely finger at me. "And before you say anything, yes. Nessie's in on it, too, and she told me to give you a good wallop if you had anything to say about that."

I can't help but smile at the thought. It's exactly what I'd expect the old woman to say. Nessie is a tough old bird. I know better than to even try to argue about her involvement, despite the danger it might put her in.

"Okay then," I say, gesturing toward the bed mats. "What say we have a pow-wow and discuss our next move. I'm going to definitely need people who are able to move about freely in town."

"I'm your gal then."

I'm pretty sure I blush at that.

"Don't get any fresh ideas, you," Trixie laughs. "You know what I mean."

We sit there for the next hour or so, discussing the chain of events that led to Angelique's death—although I still keep the exact nature of our meeting, as well as Morris Grant's presence —out of it as much as I can. Although I'm still not sure what part Morris played in the murder, if any, I still have to assume what I was told by both of him and Angelique is true. And that he's one of the good guys. Besides, the need to keep state secrets has been ingrained in me since first joining the Navy. The secrecy of a potential list of communist revolutionaries has to be maintained, no matter what, until I can secure it and get it back to the right people.

"But what about this list I've heard about?" Trixie asks, as if reading my mind.

I forgot the fact that she overheard the Red agents talking about Angelique's connection with the French secret service, the American visitor, and the list. It's one of the main reasons the beautiful Hungarian was so ready to believe in my innocence. She has no love for the Soviet Union, especially after their occupation of her country since the war and their propensity to send Hungarian dissenters to the work camps in the icy fields of Siberia. No one hates or distrusts the Russian government more than her.

Still, despite having heard the Reds talking about it, I don't want her getting involved in that side of things. It's one thing to help me prove my innocence. It's another thing entirely to get involved in espionage with trained killers prowling about. And while I think the two things are more than likely connected, it's best to keep everyone as in-the-dark as I can about that end of things.

"Don't get caught up on that list," I say, lighting up a cigar. "Right now, let's just focus on..."

"Oh, no you don't," Trixie says, standing up from her spot and giving me the business end of her index finger. "Don't you try to shield me, Joe Thacker. Those lugs seemed to think you knew something about that list...that you were part of some spy ring or something. So I want to know what's going on."

Crap. There goes my plan to keep her out of the loop.

I give Malik a look and nod for him to vamoose for a bit. With a roll of his eyes, he scrambles to his feet and moves off into the darkness, with Moe hot on his heels. When I believe he's outside of hearing range, I lean forward.

"Okay. I'll tell you what I know," I whisper, wanting to at least keep the kid out of it, if I can. The more he knows, the more danger he'll be in, and I'd never be able to live with myself if anything happened to him. "Angelique is…" I pause, then shake my head. "…*was*, a spy for the French SDECE, their counter-espionage agency." I shrug when her eyes widen at the news. "Yeah, I know. Threw me for a loop, too. Anyway, she told me that the cargo I just smuggled from Cuba contained top secret information in it."

"What was it?"

I shrug. "No idea. And the weird thing is, I packed the crates up myself. I know every single piece of merchandise in them. There was no list. No paperwork of any kind. Just booze and candy for the shop."

"So, do you have any theories?"

"Not a one. I'm pretty sure Angelique was going to tell me more about it, but I passed out before she could."

"And the American agent?"

We are quickly moving into uncomfortable territory, especially after Morris shot Winston so coldly in the woods earlier. My old pal obviously has no qualms about killing, and the last place I want Trixie is in his cross hairs.

"I don't know anything about him."

She throws me a withering, though amused, look that always works. I have no resistance against it.

"Okay. So, he's an old friend of mine from the war. Haven't seen him in years. Then all of a sudden, he pops up at Angelique's and tells me he's with the CIA."

"Do you think he could have killed Angelique? Framed you?"

"Once again, no clue. The man I used to know would never do anything like that, but ten years is a long time to change a man. No telling what he's capable of now."

She nods at that and stares off into space, as if in deep thought. After a moment, she looks over at me.

"So where do you think that list is now?"

I belt out a frustrated little laugh. "You are pitching a no-hitter today, Trixie." I raise my hands. "Have absolutely no idea. What's worse, Monday Renot confiscated the cargo the moment I stepped on the island. He had the full support of Governor Lagrange. In hindsight, knowing he's in bed with those KGB stooges, I bet it wasn't a coincidence. I'm sure the cargo's been searched. If there was some kind of top secret list in there, they would have found it by now."

Trixie shakes her head. "I'm not so sure about that. The way that Vladimir and Alexi were talking, I think they believe you might have it on you, or something."

Vladimir? Alexi? So Trix is on first a name basis with these Bozos?

I tamp down the flaring jealousy and make a big show of patting myself down and looking confused. "Um, no, not here. Or here. Or here. Nope, as far as I know, I don't have it either." I bite down on the cigar in my mouth. "Look, Trix, I think we might be barking up the wrong tree here. You're too focused on all the spy stuff, when it could be something a lot simpler than that."

She bites at her lower lip, thinking over what I've just said, and shakes her head. "No, no. I don't think so. The pieces seem to be fitting pretty well. A couple of KGB mooks show up to the island shortly after a CIA agent with a top secret list you're hauling back from Cuba, then Angelique, who turns out to be a spy, too, no less, ends up dead in a perfect frame job against you. Sounds more likely than anything else."

"What about Jacques?"

She blinks at me. "Huh? The Candyman? No way. He'd never kill Angelique."

"Even if he thought she was doing the voodoo bebop with my friend, Morris?"

That seems to get her attention. "The Candyman knew about your friend?"

I nod into the darkness, where I assume Malik is still lurking. "According to Malik, Morris was a frequent guest in the Lagrange bungalow. Says Jacques even let him inside a few times."

"Really? Do you think he might work for the SDECE as well?"

"Honestly? Who knows? I never imagined Angelique being involved in an outfit like that either, so I really am totally lost here."

"Either way, looks like we've come right back to the list, doesn't it?"

I think about it, and I can't find an argument against it. For a minute, I wonder if there's a jealousy element to the murder. But the Candyman has never been the jealous type. Of course, most of that comes from the fact that there's not a man on the island who would dare try to two-time it with his old lady. So maybe jealousy was never an issue, until Morris arrived.

But then why let Morris into his house? That's what isn't making any sense. And if the Candyman knew about Morris— knew about our friendship—why didn't he tell me he met him?

Unless, he's involved in the spy thing, too.

I shake my head as I stand to my feet and run my hand through my hair, before putting my captain's cap on again.

"Okay, Trix, you win. I can't think of a single other possible motive for the murder. It's got to be that list."

"So the only thing I can think of now is we've got to find it," she says. "And we've got to find it before the Russians or the Governor does."

I nod.

"Malik? You still there, kid?"

He's been quiet the whole time Trixie and I have been talking. I'm kind of worried.

"Um, yeah. Still here." The boy sounds groggy, like he's been sleeping the entire time. I forgot the fact that his sleep was interrupted by Trixie's arrival. I'm not sure how long we were asleep—hard to tell time in a pitch black cave—but it could only have been a few hours.

I hear his feet scraping against the stone floor, just as he appears in the firelight, rubbing his eyes and yawning. Moe is at rest on the boy's shoulders, his tail wrapped around the boy's neck and his eyes closed tight.

"Okay, here's the plan." I look over at Trixie. "You need to head back to Port Lucine and just go about your daily routine. Act normal. And just wait. If I need you, I'll send Malik to you with a message."

"Now wait just a minute, mister…"

I raise up a hand, cutting her off. "Don't argue with me on this. I have a plan, but it won't work if you're under suspicion. I need you to be exactly where you always are…at Nessie's, doing your songbird thing."

"And what will you be doing in this plan of yours?"

I throw her my most rakish grin. "What I do best, Sweetheart. Making it up as I go along."

CHAPTER 14

I spend pretty much all of the next day doing two things: trekking through swampy, muck-covered jungle and hiding out until dark. The first task was hard and grueling. The second, hot, sweaty, and uncomfortable. But my hiding space under the overturned, wood-rotten dinghy on the edge of Crescent Beach, just a few miles south of town, hasn't been without its comforts. Although I haven't been able to smoke in the confined space, Malik provided me with a bottle of rum, which has kept me company through the heat of the day.

I've been cautious about over-drinking, of course. The last thing I need is to stumble into the Customs Office in the dead of night in a drunken haze. But it's given me something to do, as I while away my time waiting for sunset and the cover of darkness.

Once night falls and the sounds of the town commerce drift to that of revelry and song, I slip from my spot and creep along the beach, hugging the edge of the jungle as I inch toward the old rickety structure that houses the St. Noel Customs Office. The building, which is little more than a few cross beams covered by four walls of corrugated metal and a tin roof, hasn't been the most heavily guarded structure around, historically. However, as I approach, I immediately spot several differences from my last visits to the place.

The first difference I notice is the chain-link fence, topped with coils of razor wire, that stretches around the property. The other new addition I spot are the two German Shepherds patrolling the grounds with their noses practically glued to the ground.

"Huh," I mutter. "Didn't expect this."

Granted, it's been nearly six months since I've found it necessary to visit old Monday's place of employment. Our mutual arrangements have pretty much nixed any need to appeal whatever inconvenient confiscations that might have otherwise occurred. But from the shiny glint of the quarter moon reflecting off the fence, I'm willing to bet it's been erected recently. Like, within 'the last couple of days' recently.

I'm willing to bet my latest smuggling run has something to do with the updated security around here, but I still have hope. If the list was in my crates, there would be little need for such measures now. I can hardly see Governor Lagrange spending more money than necessary to upgrade security for a Customs Office that's rarely used. Because of that, it seems to me that there's good reason to believe that whatever was in my cargo that interests so many people hasn't been found yet.

That's the good news.

The bad news is that while circumventing the fence should be a piece of cake, dealing with the dogs is something else entirely. Maybe someone like my pal Morris would just shoot them and be done with it, but despite my protests to the contrary when it comes to Moe, I'm an animal lover. I don't hurt animals. Ever. And the watch dogs are going to present a particularly difficult obstacle for me because of it.

After all, it's not their fault their master is a greedy, no-good dictator in bed with commies. They're just working for their next meal and maybe a good pat on the head. I can't blame them for that.

If I hadn't left Moe in Malik's care for this little excursion, I maybe could have used him as a distraction for the mutts. But I didn't, so I can't, and I figure I'll just have to improvise when the time comes.

Still huddled up against a stand of palm trees, I peer left and right to ensure the proverbial coast is clear. Although Port Lucine is a bit further away than the pier on which the *Dream* is moored, the sound of calypso permeates the air in crisp tones from steel drums and Trixie's unmistakable voice. I can picture it now, her on stage, sensually gyrating to the beat of the drums, her luscious red lips pressed against the microphone, and every red-blooded male in the joint totally fixated on her every move. Her every word. Her every breath.

Which is a good thing for me. It gives me plenty of time to do what I need to do now.

I dash over to the fence, keeping as low as I can. The guard dogs, by my calculation, are on the other side of the property. Once they catch my scent, it shouldn't take them long to track me down, so I'm going to have to move quickly.

I pull off my jacket and toss it over the razor wire, then step back before taking a leap and clambering up the chain link. Once at the apex, I reposition the jacket, making sure its leather fabric is sufficient protection against the barbs, and I climb over, dropping to the ground on the other side once I've recovered the coat.

That's the easy part. It's the dogs that cause me the most apprehension. They're the wild cards in this little poker game of mine, impossible to predict and viciously efficient—if well-trained.

Not wanting to press my luck, I run over to the building and lean my back against the corrugated metal as I stop and listen. For a moment, I think I hear some snuffling around the corner, like a snout pressed against the ground, sniffing out intruders, but I can't be certain. Fortunately, there's a cracked ventilation window directly above me. I won't have to peek around to see if I'm right or not.

Taking a few steps back, I get a running jump, and scramble up the wall until my fingers find purchase on the lip of the window. There's a low grumble behind me. As I hang from my fingertips, I crane my head and see one of the German Shepherds staring up at me. Its fangs are bared. Drool hangs from its black lips.

Realizing my feet are only a couple of feet off the ground, I struggle to push the window open. The old white paint is chipped around the frame. Though it's open by a few inches, it's obvious the window hasn't moved in years. It's stuck in place, and I don't have a secure enough purchase to get the leverage needed to force it open any farther without outright breaking the glass.

The dog doesn't appear to be the slightest bit put-off by my precarious dilemma. Before I can react, it lunges forward, taking the few feet necessary to leap into the air and grab hold of my ankle with its vice-like maw. I kick at the dog with my free leg, sending it rolling to the ground with a yelp, but the noise only draws the attention of the second animal, who is now bounding around the corner directly at me.

With only seconds on my side, I pull on the window with all my strength. I feel the frame give a fraction of an inch, bolstering my resolve. I strain, pulling for dear life, until finally, the frame creaks and the window lifts out from the building with ease. I then pull myself through the opening and slip into the building, just as the two snarling beasts snap at my heels.

The dogs bark in rage outside the safe confines of the building, stopping only to allow themselves a frustrated growl here and there, to let me know with no uncertainty that they'll still be there when I decide to leave. I file their warnings away in the 'I'll cross that bridge...' category and turn my attention to the task at hand.

The Customs Office is just a six hundred square foot rectangular building with two army surplus desks and chairs near the garage doors up front and four eight-foot-high shelves that stretch all the way from the front of the building to the back in two parallel rows. There's a small storage room in the back, locked with a padlock, for the more valuable contraband. A room Monday affectionately, and maybe ironically, calls 'The Vault.'

Turning on the army flashlight Malik provided me, I move toward the desk to start my systematic search for anything that might be useful to my personal investigation. My key goal is to locate my cargo in hopes of discovering the top secret information, but I'm also hoping I can find something that might clear my name. Assuming that Monday Renot is in on the plot, he might have some sort of documentation that can help my case.

I step to Monday's desk and begin by scouring the paperwork and reports covering the ink blotter. Besides a few memos from the Governor's office, almost all of what I examine are inventory reports and manifests from the various cargo ships coming into and out of Port Lucine within the last six months. There's a memorandum from Governor Lagrange about *me*. However, it's simply the orders that brought the customs agent and the porter to my slip three days ago. There's nothing sinister about it at all. As a matter of fact, the wording is your typical bureaucratic fare, which leads me to believe that Monday has absolutely no idea about the true nature of the cargo—or the reasons for which the Governor wanted it confiscated.

That doesn't surprise me. Monday might be a greedy S.O.B., but he's got no love for the Governor, and a communist takeover of the island would almost certainly interfere with the various 'side businesses' he's involved in. I figured he wasn't part of any Red conspiracy. This memo seems to clinch it.

Having exhausted everything on top of the desk, I turn my attention to the drawers, moving through them swiftly, but finding only more papers, a carton of smokes, and a handful of whiskey bottles I suspect have come directly from some of my previous shipments.

I switch to the second desk, more than likely occupied by the porter, Lamont Kingston. On the surface, everything checks out pretty much the same as Monday's desk. Then, I attempt to open the largest drawer at the bottom right of the desk and find it locked. By itself, it's not exactly a surprise. However, given my circumstances, I find it suspicious enough to warrant more extreme measures to search it.

I scan the top of the desk again, find a sturdy silver letter opener, and shove the point into the top of the drawer. With a few nudges, I hear the latch in the drawer snap, and I pull the opener out with a triumphant grunt.

When I look inside the drawer, I instantly think I under-stand why it was locked. Like with Monday's desk, there are stacks of folders in here. However, the difference between the two is the Nagant M1895 revolver—one of the favorite sidearms of choice for Soviet soldiers back in the war—that sits on top of it all.

I stare at the weapon for a few long seconds, wondering what it means. Kingston's possession of such a firearm wouldn't be suspicious in and of itself, given his position. Lots of ships have come and gone through this port for the past few decades—including Russian naval vessels. Soldiers and sailors of any number of nationalities tend to sell off valuable goods, when on shore leave, to willing buyers. Lamont's position as porter would put him in the perfect place to get first dibs on such transactions.

But given the nature of my current mess, I'm having a hard time believing the Soviet firearm is a coincidence.

Since I'm already wanted for murder, and I'm now in the process of committing burglary, I have no qualms about scooping the gun up and sticking it down the waistband in the back of my pants for safekeeping before concealing it with my jacket. I then begin perusing the file folders, sifting through them one by one, until my eye lands on one that confirms my suspicions.

The folder, near the bottom of the drawer, is labeled with the familiar red and yellow hammer and sickle symbol and Cyrillic lettering I take from context alone to translate as 'Top Secret' or some other spook nonsense. With shaking fingers, I open the folder. Though the words on the pages are indecipherable to me, the photos and the subsequent meaning are not.

The folder is filled with what looks like dossiers on the various important people on St. Noel—including Angelique and myself. The Governor, the Candyman, Nessie, and almost every adult individual of any political or social standing on the island, all complete with recent photographs, are contained within. There are a few hand-scrawled pencil markings here and there on the margins, which I assume were made by Lamont Kingston.

So the scrawny little mook is a Red spy. Who'd have thought?

Even more unsettling, it appears that he's been documenting facts about us for several years now. Keeping tabs on us, gauging our loyalties.

I grind my teeth at the thought. Next time I see him, Lamont Kingston's going to have fewer teeth in that commie-loving head of his. I promise myself that much. My life might not be worth spit, and I might get myself killed by a mob of voodoo-practicing locals, but before I take the big sleep, I'm going to see that Kingston gets at least a knuckle sandwich or two.

I close the desk drawer, leaving it slightly ajar intentionally, and I turn to the shelves full of wooden crates, wrapped parcels, and other knick-knacks confiscated by the customs agents. There aren't that many. Maybe a total of eleven or twelve items.

Like I said, St. Noel isn't a big attraction in the Caribbean, so there's not much contraband for Monday to deal with. It's good news for me, because it means it doesn't take me long to peruse the labels of each item and discover what I've already suspected is true. My cargo isn't among the confiscated treasures on the shelves.

I turn to the back of the building and look at the locked door of the Vault. I roll my eye with a sigh. It's not that the vault is a formidable obstacle to anyone determined to break into the place. Getting in is going to be easy enough. A simple crowbar to the padlock and any burglar worth his salt would be in, free and clear. The problem is, I've heard enough of Monday's drunken boasting to know that it's going to be the most dangerous part of my venture tonight.

You see, the space is reserved for the most precious of all contraband. Stuff so valuable, in fact, that the Governor spent a little more money on the bells and whistles for it—literally. Even though most of St. Noel is still crawling its way into the twentieth century, the vault is the only structure on the island with an alarm system. It's loud enough to alert the entire island. As a matter of fact, the alarm is attached to the same loudspeakers used for our hurricane warning system. I have no idea how to circumvent it or shut it off.

No matter what, the moment I break into it, the entire island will know I'm here.

CHAPTER 15

O f course, I suspected I'd face this eventuality, and I figured I'd just have to deal with it, but there was a part of me hoping Monday would have made my life easier by simply placing my cargo on the easy-to-get-to shelves.

Taking a frustrated breath, I grab a crowbar from its hook above a nearby tool bench and step over to the Vault's door.

The way I figure it, the moment I trip the alarm, I'll only have a good five to ten minutes to search the room and get out, before the entire town comes running down the lane with torches and pitchforks. It's not as much time as I'd like, but it'll do. Though I've never been inside, the Vault appears to be small—no larger than a six-by-twelve-foot cell, and I've been in plenty of those in my time.

I set the military flashlight on a desk, illuminating the door, and I plunge the crowbar into the padlock's loop. Once firmly inserted, I heave. After a moment of exerted effort, the iron loop snaps open, sending the lock crashing to the floor.

Taking yet another deep breath, I grab the flashlight, steel myself, reach out, and open the Vault's wooden door. As expected, the moment it swings open, I hear the mechanical cranking sound of a rotor above the building, just before the civil defense siren begins to wail out into the night. The sound is deafening. But judging by the whines and howls of the canines outside, it's even worse for them. Perhaps the alarm will be a blessing in disguise, as far as my escape goes.

But I don't have time to think about that. Right now, I have work to do.

I step inside the room and stop in my tracks, when I spot two distinctively different things. The first is the wooden remains of four crates that have been smashed to pieces by what I can only imagine to be a sledgehammer/crowbar combo. The bottles of booze have been smashed against the concrete floor and have exploded into hundreds of razor-sharp shards. The acidic stench of spilled alcohol permeates the air inside. The candy packages have been opened as well, and all the individually wrapped treats are scattered throughout the room, as if thrown in a fit of frustrated rage.

I'm not certain they found what they were looking for, but by the mess, I can almost guarantee they didn't. And if they did, by some miracle, it was in the very last possible place it could have been.

But the state of my crates and cargo isn't the most unnerving thing I find in the room. The second thing that catches my eye is a single wicker chair sitting off to the right, by the northwest wall. Blood-covered ropes rest unused on the floor beside its legs. Next to it, there's a large maroon spot staining the floor under the chair, and there's a ghastly amount of dried blood spattering the wall behind it.

In my time during the war, I had the good, but also nightmare-inducing, fortune to be part of an operation in the Pacific Theater where we rescued more than two dozen allied soldiers held captive by the Japanese. As I toured the camp after the mission was over, I came across rooms similar to this, stained with various shades of crimson, almost painting the walls with the blood of tortured service men.

Torture rooms always have the same look. Always smell the same. And always ignite a rage in my gut that could set the entire jungle on fire with just a glare.

Someone's been tortured here. And from the amount of blood I'm seeing, I don't think it's possible they survived. Of course, two questions come to mind as I stare at the mess in front of me. Who was the sad sack that sat in that chair, and why was it necessary to torture them?

I look from the smashed crates to the chair and connect a few dots.

Whoever it was, the torturers thought they might know the whereabouts of the secret list. They brought the person here, along with the contraband, to coerce answers from them as they searched. At least, that's the best guess I can come up from the scene. It also tells me something else. Whoever's behind all this means business. I can definitely see them killing to get what they want, so the idea of them offing Angelique and framing me is starting to make a lot more sense.

Except, why let me live? Why frame me? I'm not part of any of this. I'm just the mug who smuggled a few boxes of liquor and candy to the island. I didn't even know about the list, until I went to have my blasted fortune told.

I always knew that voodoo hooey was bad news.

I back out of the Vault, taking a look at my watch. No more than two minutes have passed from the time I cracked open the door to now. I'm making good...

The sound of an engine heading this way brings my optimism to a screeching halt. Only two people on the island have motor cars—the Candyman and Governor Lagrange. Neither one of them will be too pleased to find me here. Given the location of the security breech, I'm guessing Monday and the Port Lucine police force are riding shotgun or are close on their heels.

It's the cars I haven't figured on, and it's those kinds of mistakes that'll lead to me becoming either a human voodoo doll or standing in front of a firing squad in Martinique. I'm not particularly keen on either of those things happening.

I turn around, getting ready to run for my life, and I find a sharp-dressed man with a gun pointed at my face. I recognize him as one of the KGB goons I tangled with at Nessie's. The one I assumed to be the leader. The same lug Trixie was chatting up, outside the drug store, on the night of the festival. *The one Morris called Alexi Krashnov,* I think.

My hands go up into the air.

The brim of his fedora is tipped low, shielding his eyes from the glare of the flashlight. His cigarette hangs limp from one corner of his grinning mouth, and it's enough to let me know what's he thinking.

He's pleased with himself.

"I figured it would be only a matter of time before you came here," Alexi says with that harsh Russian accent of his. "So I wait. And wait. My comrades...they say I'm crazy for staking this place out, but I knew you'd come. My father always taught me, while hunting bear, all you need is little honey and great deal of patience." He waves the barrel of the gun in a circle. "Turn around."

I can still hear the car engine speeding down the lane. It won't be long before whoever it is gets here.

"Why? So you can shoot me in the back?"

He laughs. "I have no need to shoot you in the back, Captain. I can just as easily do it between your eyes."

There's a mental flash of Angelique lying dead on her

bamboo floor, a round hole perfectly placed in the center of her forehead.

"So, it *was* you..."

I feel my blood begin to boil, but he interrupts before I can finish my accusation.

"I said, turn around." He removes his cigarette from his lips with his free hand and nods his head in the direction of the approaching car. "We don't have a lot of time."

So the Ruskie doesn't want to get caught here either. That's interesting.

With no recourse, I do as he says and turn my back to him. He steps up close behind me, reaches his hand around, slipping into the interior of my jacket and pulling my .45 from its shoulder holster.

"There," he says, stepping back again. "I just wanted to relieve you of your weapon."

I obey, forcing my face to remain as neutral as possible. He obviously doesn't know about the Russian-issued revolver I've scored from Lamont's desk drawer. I aim to keep it that way for as long as possible.

"Now what?"

We hear car tires crunch to a stop along the gravel drive out by the fence's gate. He nods to the Vault. "Get in," he says. "Take a seat."

I shudder as memories of the blood-crusted chair, and the torture that's taken place there, spring to mind.

"And for God's sake, turn off that light and be quiet."

The man's accent slips with that last comment. It sounds more Brooklyn than Russian.

"Go!" He cocks the hammer of his gun back to let me know he means business.

Once again, I comply, backing into the old storage room without a word. I can only watch as the man shuts the door on me. I can hear him just outside, fumbling with something metal, then the click of a lock being placed on the door's latch.

Has Alexi replaced the padlock I broke? But why? Why not just turn me over to the police? They all seem to be in on it anyway.

A moment later, the alarm is shut down and the howling dogs calm down. I press my ear against the Vault's door and hear the garage doors rumble open before several people storm inside. Shouts. Angry voices. Alexi's thick accent has returned, as he's questioned by someone. The voices get louder as they draw closer to the Vault. I hear keys in the padlock and my blood goes cold.

I pull the Nagant from my waistband and point it at the door. The gun has seven 7.62 millimeter rounds. Should be more than enough to take care of everyone outside. If my aim isn't as lousy as it normally is. But even if it is, I'll at least take a few of them out before I'm mowed down myself. It's a crappy excuse for a consolation prize, but I'll take it. Just a couple fewer Reds the world will have to deal with in the long run.

A fair trade, I think.

But whoever's trying to open the door suddenly stops. I hear the key sliding out of the lock and the men continue their heated debate. Among the people out there, I can easily make out Alexi's voice and another Russian. I think I can just make out Monday's weasely voice among the mix, as well as Governor Lagrange and Chief Armad.

It seems like the gang's all here. So the big question is why they're not all beating down the door to turn the screws to me, the same way they did the last tenant in this butcher shop.

Did Alexi's accent really change? Or was that my imagination?

It's a fair question. My heart is racing so fast, the blood is pounding in my ears, making sounds all cloudy—if that makes any sense. In the excitement, I could have easily just been hearing things. But the KGB man sure sounded like a New York for a split second. Besides, how many communists would refer to God in such a cavalier manner? They're state-mandated atheists, for crying out loud.

The men outside are still arguing, but their voices are drawing farther away. They're moving back to the front of the warehouse now. I let out the breath I was unaware I was holding, but I'm careful not to relax too much. This ain't over. Besides, even if the Governor, the Chief, and Monday beat tracks, that still leaves Alexi and his *comrades* to contend with.

I hear the garage door close, and I hold my breath again, listening for movement. No one speaks. No footsteps echo past the door. For a moment, I think I'm finally alone. Then, a key clinks into the padlock, and I hear it pop open. I step to the side of the door, keeping myself out of view, and I ready the gun I still have clutched in my hand.

The door creaks open, and the light of a flashlight sweeps into the vault.

"All right, Thacker," Alexi says. "You can come out now."

Keeping quiet, I don't move an inch.

"Thacker?"

Still nothing.

A hand holding a gun very similar to my own sweeps through the door and points in my general direction. I duck down, careful not to make a sound.

"I know you're in here. There's no way you could get out."

He steps through the door, only to find my gun pointed at his head.

"Hiya, Red," I say, grinning like the Cheshire Cat. "You can lower your gun now."

"How did..." He lowers his weapon, then he nods in understanding. "So, you found Mr. Kingston's... How do you Americans say it? His piece? His rod?"

"You'd only say that if your name was Edward G. Robinson." I stand up to face him. "But then, you'd know that, given that you're American yourself."

He makes a good show of acting surprised by my accusation, but I see right through it.

"Don't even try," I say, taking a step away from him for a better vantage point of the warehouse behind him. Just as I thought. No one else is in the building. "What are you? CIA? FBI?" I give his gun a nod. "Oh, and you can drop that *piece* now. You're not going to get the chance to use it anytime soon."

His gun clatters to the floor.

"I do not know what you..." He starts to deny it, but I shake my head.

"Don't even try to lie." I gesture with my gun, silently ordering him to back out of the Vault's door. He does so, and I follow him into the warehouse area. "You're good. I'll give you that. Your accent is nearly flawless." I keep directing him backward with the barrel of my gun. "Except when you get a little excited. Then, you slip back to your Brooklyn roots." I pause. "Let me guess, your folks were Russian immigrants. You grew up hearing and speaking the language."

He stares at me for a long moment, as if trying to figure out how to best handle my interrogation, then finally, he just shrugs in resignation.

"You got me," he says, completely dropping the fake accent. "And I work for the FBI. On direct orders from Director Hoover."

His admission floors me. Anyone who's got old J. Edgar's ear is someone to take very seriously.

"Did you get rid of everyone?" I ask out of the blue. "Are they coming back?"

He shakes his head. "They won't be coming back tonight. I

told them I'd accidentally set off the alarm while doing surveillance for you. They weren't happy about it, but they believed me. Left me here to keep watch until dawn."

Satisfied with his answer, I nod over to the desks. "Well, then, how about you and I take a load off and having ourselves a little chat, shall we?"

CHAPTER 16

"What I'm about to tell you can't go any further than this building," the G-Man says.

I've just realized I don't know his real name, and I highly doubt I ever will. I nod my understanding.

"Sure," I say. "All I'm interested in is finding a way to clear my name."

"That, my friend, might be more difficult to do than you think." He sits back in the office chair. I allow him to light up a cigarette, and he takes a long pull from it before continuing. "Even I don't know who killed Angelique Lagrange."

That catches me by surprise.

"You mean, you guys didn't do it? I've been going on the notion than the KGB was behind the murder all this time."

He shakes his head. "Neither Vladimir nor I had anything to do with it," he says, exhaling a stream of smoke through his nostrils. "But there are other KGB agents here on the island that could have done it."

"Like who?"

"I'm not sure. That's what I'm here to find out."

I lean back in my chair and give him a good look over. The

man is perfectly nondescript. Average height. Average build. Dark hair. Dark eyes. Dark suit with a white hat. Perfect look for a spy, but I'm not sure I'm buying his story.

"Okay, maybe you need to start from the beginning. What's your connection to all this? How'd you get involved?"

"That's classified. I'm not authorized to share that with you."

"I'm the guy with the gun." The barrel is pointed directly at his gut. "Make an exception. With everything going on with me right now, I'm not in much of a mood for the cloak and dagger routine."

He grinds his cigarette butt in the ashtray on his desk and exhales up into the air. "Okay, but by telling you all this, you're agreeing to be part of the operation. All of it. 'Til the end."

"In my current predicament, I'm not sure the 'end' is all that far away. Go for it."

"Your funeral," he says, lighting up another smoke. "It started with the arrest of the real Alexi Krashnov at the Washington National Airport a year and a half ago. We had word he'd come to the U.S. planning on meeting with some Soviet sympathizers to help organize a series of revolutions in the Caribbean islands. We busted him before he even made it out the doors. And, after a few weeks of some of Hoover's hospitality, he decided to open up and share everything we wanted to know."

I shudder, considering J. Edgar's warm and friendly disposition. I kind of feel sorry for the KGB mook.

"Once we had key intel and learned that none of his Western contacts had ever seen Alexi's face, Director Hoover reached out to me and asked me to assume his identity and proceed with the real Alexi's itinerary as planned. Along the way, I met up with several sleeper agents living inside the

United States, and eventually I made my way to Cuba, where I was assigned to work with Vladimir Petrovic and Boris Usilov, who you met at the bar the other night."

"And no one suspected you of being an American spy?"

"Not that I'm aware of. Everything was going great until Morris Grant showed up in Cuba. We were supposed to receive correspondence from our contact here on St. Noel. A list of highly interested individuals who live in the Caribbean, who were open to a communist revolution. It was the holy grail for me. The whole reason I was sent on my mission to begin with. If I could get my hands on that list, we could shut down these revolts before they even got started."

I nod, understanding what happened next. "But Morris intercepted the correspondence before you guys did."

"Exactly."

"So what was the problem? Morris is a US spy. He would have gotten the list to the right people. From my understanding, he only ended up sending it here to St. Noel when he got spooked by you and your pals."

The G-Man sighs. "This is going to sound petty," he says. "But the truth is, the FBI and CIA don't exactly trust each other. And I personally don't trust Morris Grant."

"You know him?"

"A little. We crossed paths a few times, especially during the war. But despite the FBI's feelings about the CIA, and my personal feelings about your friend, the higher ups with the KGB were more concerned than any of us. They ordered us to track the list down and the agent who had stolen it. I had no choice if I wanted to keep my cover intact."

"Okay. So Morris finds a way off Cuba, but not before somehow getting the list to the port in Havana and arranging for me to smuggle it back here." I shake my head, confused. "I don't get it. Why not just ship it the same way to the U.S.?

Why didn't he just send it to Miami, where his bosses could just pick it up at the harbor? Why smuggle it back into the Caribbean?"

"That's what's had me stumped for a while now, too," he says. "Makes no sense to me at all."

I shrug that particular mystery off and continue. "Morris makes his way here, and you follow him a few days later, right?"

"At first, we had no idea where he'd gone. Then we got word from an agent on St. Noel that he'd been spotted."

"Which agent? Kingston?"

He shakes his head. "No. Kingston apparently is pretty low level. Stationed here to keep tabs on the comings and goings of people here. I doubt it was him, though he might have notified his superior on the island about Morris's arrival. He would have been in a perfect position to recognize him once he came ashore."

So Lamont Kingston isn't the only resident Russian spy on St. Noel?

I can't wrap my head around it. It's such a tiny island with a very small population. It's difficult to imagine anybody being in league with the Reds. Then again, I'm still not sure I trust my new *comrade*. For all I know, this whole thing could be an elaborate scheme to learn if I have the list or not.

"So, who's the head honcho on the island?"

"Excuse me?"

"Who's in charge? I'm assuming it's Governor Lagrange."

"Why do you think that?"

"Because you fellas met with him the moment you came to the island. Because he seems to be all over this. Even ensured my cargo was impounded so it could be searched for the list."

Alexi shakes his head. "You'd be wrong. *We* didn't meet with Lagrange when we first arrived. I did. Privately."

"I'm not sure I see the distinction."

"Governor Lagrange is extremely anti-communist," he explains. "He has sent numerous letters to the French government asking for assistance in regards to rumors he's been hearing in the region. He's been fighting a one-man war against the communists for the past seven years, in fact."

"Anton Lagrange? Are you sure you're not confusing him with his brother?"

The G-man smiles. "I'm certain. That's why I went to meet with him. Besides you, he's the only one on the island who knows my true purpose here. He's been helping me every step of the way. And yes, he's responsible for confiscating your contraband, but that was on *my* request."

"And the torture chamber in there? Who'd you guys beat to a bloody pulp to find out where the list is?"

"That wasn't us either. We were going to go through the crates on the night of Angelique Lagrange's murder, but all hell broke loose after she was discovered." His hands shook as he lit up another cigarette. The guy was obviously quite the chain smoker. "By the time we finally got to the Customs Office to have a look, we found the room just as you did."

I'm not sure I believe him here, either. Sounds awfully convenient that he's just as in the dark about this whole mess as I am.

"So, once again, who's pulling the strings?" I ask. "Who's the big man on this island's KGB campus?"

"That's just it. We don't know. We receive our orders in coded messages delivered to our rooms at Nessie's. We've never met the head agent here."

The cynical part of me finds it hard to believe, but the side of my brain that knows how the system works gets it. It's Intelligence 101. Never let the right hand know what the feet are doing while the left hand ties a bow in the hat for the head.

The fewer people in the loop, the better it is for security of any operation.

Still though, it's such a small island.

"Do you have any suspects for Mr. Big?"

He offers a brief nod.

"Well? Who's at the top of that list?"

The G-Man fidgets in his chair, tapping the ash from his cigarette, and avoiding looking me in the face. I start to get a mental picture of something I don't like, and I stand from my chair in protest.

"You don't mean…"

"Yes," He says. His voice is barely a whisper as he says it. "The bet among us was that you were the best option. Especially after you were discovered with the body of a French spy. My associates posited that she discovered your secret and tried to take you out with knockout drops, but you took her out before she could interrogate you."

I sit back down, the wind taken out of my sails. The theory does make a certain kind of sense. I can see why anyone with the background information the KGB goons have might make the argument. Then again, I can make the same case for Morris.

"Besides me, any other suspects?"

"No one in particular. Then again, my associates aren't as interested as I am in discovering his identity. They're here for the list and that's all they're focused on."

Once again, we're right back to where we started. The blasted list. No matter what I do, I can't get away from it. The list is the key.

But where is it?

I glance down at my watch. It's getting late. Or early, depending on your perspective. For now, I'm pretty sure I've exhausted everything I can from the undercover FBI man, while doing pretty well at keeping just what I know hazy. I still don't trust him. A Russian could just as easily fake a Brooklyn accent as an American could a Moscow one.

"All right," I say, standing to my feet. I motion for him to do the same. "Time to lock you in the Vault."

"Wait, what?"

"You want to keep your cover intact, don't you?"

He nods.

"Well, I've made a general mess here tonight. I've stolen a gun, ransacked desks, and broken the lock to the Vault. You might have replaced it, but it won't take along for someone to see it's not the same one that Monday bought. That means there's been an intruder here. An intruder you failed to see or apprehend."

"Okay."

"Now, how's that going to look if you're just standing here when Monday and Lamont show up in the morning?"

I can practically see understanding dawning on the G-Man's face.

"And that also means, I'm truly sorry."

"For what?" he asks.

I rear my right hand back and swing it as hard as I can against his jaw. He stumbles back, holding his now bleeding lip with his hands.

"...the heck did you do that for?" he shouts at me.

I grin. "It's just something I would do to any Red spy I would meet. If I didn't slug you, people would get suspicious. Trust me."

"Uh-huh," he mumbles, glaring at me from under the brim of his fedora. But he keeps a level head and starts making his way to the back of the warehouse.

"One more thing," I say, as he steps into the Vault and turns around to face me. He's now got his handkerchief out and is dabbing it gently at the cut on his lip. "How are those coded orders delivered?"

"Some kid," he replies. "Brings it up in a plain white envelope. Always early in the morning. Before dawn usually."

"You ever catch the kid's name?"

"No. But he seems pretty close to Nessie. I see him at the hotel almost every night."

Malik, I think. The street rat has his hands in almost every dirty pocket in town. I love the kid, but he's going to be the death of me yet.

"Okay. It's a place to start."

"Are you seriously going to try to find out who the chief agent is?"

"Seems like I'm going to have to, aren't I?" I begin to shut the Vault's door, then stop when it's about four inches from closing fully. "Seems to me that whoever he is, he's the best chance I've got at clearing my name and finding that stupid list."

"It's also the quickest way for you to get a bullet to the back of your head, too, Captain."

I shrug the statement off. "The way I see it, that's pretty much inevitable at this point. Might as well try to accomplish something useful while I wait for the bullet with my name on it."

With that, I close the door and use the replacement lock to seal the G-Man in. I then turn toward the window in which I first entered the Customs Office and prepare to make good my escape.

CHAPTER 17

It's three in the morning when I slip out of the Customs Office. I'm on my guard, keeping a wary eye out for the watch dogs. They've been quiet since the alarm was shut down, and I'm not sure where they might be lurking, but I'm sure they're around here somewhere.

I don't have time to deal with them at the moment either. The sun will be coming up in less than three hours, and I still have one more stop to make before I've got to head back to the smuggler's cave. A very important stop.

Crouching low, I shuffle over to the fence, planning on scrambling over the way I came in. But as I pass the gate, I can't believe my luck. It's still open, and I realize they must have left it that way so that Alexi could leave freely when he was finished keeping lookout for me. For a brief moment, I wonder if the gate was open all this time, and I kick myself for not checking when I broke in earlier. That would have made things stupidly simple, but then, that's not exactly the way things work for me most of the time.

Taking a quick look over my shoulder for any signs of the

dogs, I run past the gate, spin around once I'm through, and close it up tight. The noise of my retreat must have been louder than I planned, because the dogs are running full throttle at me, saliva oozing from their lips. They leap at the fence when they see me, but they can't get through, making them angrier than they ever were before.

"Better luck next time," I say, tipping my cap at them and sprinting away toward the jungle. I hear them howling at me as I run, but I ignore them. I have too much on my mind. Too many conflicting ideas and possibilities to process. The G-Man's account of everything makes a lot of sense to me, but it's thrown several notions I've had right out the door. So has what I found in the Customs Office.

The main thing is that the players are all mixed up now. I find myself realizing that I don't know who any of them really are.

I suspected Lagrange, the tyrannical Governor of St. Noel, to be in bed with the Reds. Instead, he vehemently opposes them, and he's been in contact with the French government for help. The man I believed to be a KGB spy turns out to possibly be an agent with the FBI. The simpleton porter that I've never paid much attention to is a really a sleeper agent for the KGB, keeping tabs on anybody who's anybody in St. Noel. Morris is CIA, but his behavior lately makes me question his loyalties. And Angelique? The biggest surprise of all. French intelligence.

No one seems to be who I think they are, and that makes me nervous. I'm beginning to question everyone now. Maybe that's a good thing when a fella is trying to clear his name for a murder rap, but it's a nightmare when you think about all the good friends you've made on the island for the last ten years, and the fact that any one of them could be a cold-blooded killer.

I'm thinking all of this as I slip through the jungle like a shadow, making my way as fast as possible to Port Lucine. It's beyond risky for me to show my face in town right now, but I'm counting on the drunken revelry so common in town and the late hour. Almost everyone will be three sheets to the wind about now, fast asleep in cozy beds or urine-filled gutters, depending on who it is.

It takes me about thirty minutes to make my way to the edge of town. Crouching down behind a palmetto bush, I allow myself a moment to catch my breath while I wait and watch. Everything is dark, except for the two gaslights along the street that illuminate most of the town. The windows of the various buildings and houses from my vantage point are dark as well. Nessie's is closed up tight and shuttered for the evening. So is the candy shop.

I force myself to be patient just a little while longer and listen. Besides the occasional cry of a macaw or a chattering monkey, everything is quiet.

Satisfied, I move out of the jungle's cover and hug the shadows, making my way through town. I take things slow, stopping every now and then to listen and wait. Eventually, I round the corner of the candy shop and steal my way toward the Candyman's house.

My stomach twists into knots as the bungalow comes into view, everything roiling inside me with a slew of conflicting emotions. Fear is dominant. The fear of Jacques catching me in the act of breaking into his place. Fear of the things he'll do to me the moment he puts his meaty paws around my neck. Fear of seeing the hurt in his eyes, over what he perceives is the greatest betrayal of his life.

That last one leads me to other emotions of sorrow, and the loss of Angelique. The loss of the Candyman's friendship.

Anger rages in my gut as well, over being accused of the murder and having to go on the lam to save my life.

I tamp all those emotions down, forcing them from my thoughts, and focusing only on what I need to do next. Taking another quick look around, I creep through the picket fence surrounding the Lagrange bungalow and onto the front porch. Like the rest of the buildings along the road, all the lights are off inside. Like most homes on the island, the windows are wide open, allowing the ocean breeze to cool the interior down during the night. The linen drapes, closing off the home from watchful eyes, flap like specters from the air flowing into the home. I can hear the ceiling fan in the living room thumping its rhythmic beat. But there're no signs of life inside. No movement of any kind.

Taking a deep breath, I turn the front door knob, knowing it won't be locked. It never is. That is the respect and fear the Lagrange household has garnered over the years. No one would dare break into their abode. The door opens at my urging, and I wince as the hinges creak in protest. I stop where I am and listen. The sound of my heartbeat thrums in my ears, but if anyone heard the door squeak open, no one's beating feet to see who's here.

Once again, I don't really expect anyone to. This time of night, the Candyman's usually out like a light, his body filled with enough rum and whiskey to put down a small elephant. His dismay over the loss of his wife more than likely has him drinking more than normal, too. I should be safe from waking him, but I'm also not prepared to take my chances.

After waiting what seems like an eternity, I move fully into the house and carefully close the door. The squeaking hinges don't seem nearly as loud now as they did before, but then, I'm prepared for it this time.

With the door closed, I creep past the foyer, into the sunken living room. Empty booze bottles and filled ash trays are scattered everywhere. Clothing, both men's and lady's, is cast aside. Buttons have been torn from shirts. Stockings lay stretched and rent. A brazier hangs precariously from the ceiling fan.

Jacques has been certainly tearing one on since his wife's death, and from some of the clothes on the floor, it would only take me one try to guess who's been helping him cope.

Oddly enough, she's the one person I've snuck into the house to visit. I just hope she's not currently sharing her master's bed, or this might get awkward really fast.

Like a ghost, I move down the north hallway until I come to the first closed door I find. I ease the knob to the left and feel the door slip open. Everything is dark inside, but there's a window across the room with a smidgeon of light from the street lamps outside slipping though the blinds. My eye quickly adjusts, and I begin to make out the layout.

Directly ahead of me lies a large canopy bed with mosquito netting surrounding the frame. A small female frame huddles fetal-style with her back to me. There's a nightstand next to the bed with a glass of water and a dog-eared paperback resting on it. An old mahogany wardrobe and a makeup desk are to my left, but I only pay attention to the woman sleeping so soundly in the bed.

Clarise. The Lagrange's maid. The Candyman's plaything. And the woman most likely responsible for framing me for murder.

I pull my .45 and slip across the room to the bed, carefully pulling the mosquito netting aside and fastening it to the tie-offs along the bedposts. The creature lying so serenely across her mattress is a vision of beauty. She's fully nude, with not so much as a thin sheet to cover her. Her caramel-colored skin glistens with sweat in the humid night. Her hair, no longer in the severe bun I saw a few days ago, is wild and unkempt. Her flower-scented fragrance wafts up into my face, nearly paralyzing me.

There's something primal about this dame. She belongs here, so near the jungle. And yet, as far as I can tell, she's in it up to the elbows, as far as my frame-job goes. I can't be soft on her. This is serious business.

I lower the barrel of my gun at her head and reach around with my free hand and cover her mouth, hard. Her eyes snap open, startled. Frightened.

"Shhhhh," I hiss. "Don't make a sound, or you'll wake up tomorrow with an extra hole in your head."

Her dreamy brown eyes widen when she sees me. Tears begin to stream down her soft, high cheekbones. But she obeys me. She doesn't struggle. Doesn't try to scream.

"Good girl." With my hand still over her mouth, I allow her enough room to roll over and face me more comfortably. Her small round breasts heave violently, as she cries silently in my hand. "Now I'm going to ask you a couple of questions. You're going to answer them. Honestly. Understand?"

She nods her head.

"Okay. I know you're the one that drugged me."

Her eyes stretch even wider, and she begins to shake her head.

"Don't try to lie." I'm getting irritated now, just thinking about that night, and her ethereal beauty is no longer having its effect on me. I'm pretty sure if she says the wrong thing, I could see myself actually putting a bullet in her head for what she's done to me. "You're the only one who could have done it. You poured my coffee. You alone handed the cup to me. It had to be you."

She tries to sniff under my hand. She blinks back her tears, then after a few heartbeats, she nods.

"Okay, so you admit it?"

She nods again.

I breathe, taking it all in. I'm finally getting real answers to all this. I feel myself trembling. The gun shakes in my hand, and I will myself steady.

"Now, I'm going to ask you another question," I whisper. "I'm going to remove my hand, so you can answer. *Quietly.*" I let that last word sink in. "You know what will happen if you get too loud, right?"

She blinks again. I feel her salty tears running down the back of my hand now. She nods her understanding yet again.

"Okay, Clarise. For the grand prize, why'd you do it? Why'd you drug me and frame me for Angelique's murder?"

I ease my hand away from her mouth, but I keep it hovering mere inches away, should I need to gag her again. Carefully, she wipes the tears from her eyes with the back of her hand. I think about offering to pull her bed sheets up, to cover her nakedness. It would be the gentlemanly thing to do. But I think better of it. Naked like she is, she's vulnerable. Open. She'll be less inclined to hide anything if she doesn't have anything to hide behind. It's cruel, I know. But then, I get the distinct impression that Clarise isn't the innocent angel I've got dancing inside my head.

The dame's got wiles. And she knows exactly how to use them.

"You gonna answer my question or not?"

I don't have time for playing games. It's fast approaching dawn. I won't stand a chance once people start waking up and going about their daily business.

"I'm sorry." Her voice is a quiet sob.

"That's not going to cut it. Apologies don't unframe me."

"It was not my idea. I had no idea…"

"No idea, what? Who's idea was it exactly?"

She sniffs, wiping her nose with the back of her hand. "It was Madam Lagrange. She told me to do it."

CHAPTER 18

"What did you say?"

She's still sobbing, but I'm impressed with how well she's controlling the volume of her voice. "Madame Lagrange. She asked me to drug you and Monsieur Grant both."

I'm wasn't expecting that response. The room begins to spin around me, as I let what she's telling me sink in. But I can't believe it. It's got to be another lie from a whore that Angelique was kind enough to take into her home. She's trying to save her own neck. Or worse, she's protecting the person who's really behind it.

I clamp my hand down over her mouth again and press the gun against her temple, leaning in and growling, "Don't lie to me, toots. I've run out of all patience, and I'm in no mood for it." I cock the hammer of the .45 back for emphasis. "You don't get any more chances."

I ease my hand up enough to give her lips room to move.

"I swear it's true. I'm not lying to you."

"Why? Why would she want to drug me?"

"Because she didn't want you there to begin with," Clarise

said. "She said you'd never approve of what she was doing, and Morris wouldn't come back to the house unless you agreed to come, too. She had no choice but to invite you."

My brain's gears are grinding, trying to make sense of all this. Angelique told me she was a spy for the French. It was a surprise, but it's hardly something I would disapprove of. Unless...

"Clarise, what was Angelique up to? You said she had you drug both me and Morris. Where did Morris go after I zonked out?"

She shook her head. "I do not know where he went. He should have been there when the Mistress was found dead, but he wasn't."

"And who killed her? Did you?"

She turns up the waterworks, shaking her head emphatically. "Oh no. I could not. Ever. Madam Lagrange was too good to me. I could never kill her."

I don't know why, but I believe her. My gut is screaming at me that the house maid is only a pawn in all this. She knows bits and pieces, but not enough to really give me all the answers.

"And this business of hers? The thing she was afraid I wouldn't like?"

She's heaving for breath in between sobs. Trying to find her voice. Compassion gets the better of me, and I reach down to the other end of the bed and pull up the silk sheets she had kicked off her in her sleep. My plan worked perfectly. She was vulnerable, all right. But far too much for my conscience.

"Thank you," she says, giving me a sad smile. "I do not know all of her plan. Just bits and pieces. Something to do with some classified information and a buyer she had lined up willing to pay a large sum for it."

I hate to admit it, but *this* is more like the Angelique that I knew and loved. She was a caring person. Larger than life. Vibrant and the life of any party. But a patriot to the French, who so many on the island have perceived to oppress them for generations? That was a little too hard to believe. It threw me, back when she revealed she worked for the SCECD. Oh, I could definitely see her doing it alright, but only for her own purposes.

When it came right down to it, Angelique Lagrange was a simple woman defined by two major characteristics. First, she was immensely passionate, protective, and loyal to her friends and loved ones. And second, she was a ruthless entrepreneur with an insatiable thirst for wealth and power. The CIA's list would be a perfect tool for pushing her beyond her current status level as St. Noel's one and only crime boss, and it would put her on the international playing field.

And she was right. I most definitely wouldn't have approved. Especially if it meant crossing my country to do it.

I look down at Clarise and nod. "Thank you," I say. "But I'm going to ask you for one more thing. You don't have to do it, but I hope you will. My life depends on it."

"You want me to confess to the police inspector from Martinique." It's not a question.

"It's the only hope I currently have of proving I didn't murder Angelique. The deck's stacked against me and…"

The bedroom door suddenly bursts open. I whirl around to see a hulking shadow rushing me from the hallway. With a roar, the Candyman lunges, smacking the gun from my hand and shoving me across the room with his powerful right arm. My head strikes the edge of the makeup desk, and brilliant flashes of light fill my vision with the impact. When I finally shake it off, I scramble to my feet, ready for a fight, and I can only gasp at what I now see.

The Candyman is standing over Clarise, who's cringing in

her bed with the sheets up around her neck. He has my gun in his hand, its barrel pointed down at her head. He looks at me with a vile grin spread across his face.

"No!" I shout.

But it's too late. He pulls the trigger. Clarise's head opens up like a piñata. Brain and blood spew out against the wall, sheets, and canopy. She goes still. Lifeless. And the Candyman turns his hate-filled eyes toward me.

"Why? Why did you..."

But before I can get the question out of my mouth, he drops the gun to the floor, and runs toward me with a roar that shakes the house. Though I see him coming, I can't get out of the way in time. He smashes into me at full sprint, sending me through the plaster wall into the next bedroom.

The room is spinning uncontrollably now. My ears are ringing. I'm disoriented, but it's worse than that. My heart is breaking, too. Why is he doing this? I can understand him being angry, if he thinks I killed his wife, but why murder Clarise?

I have no time to ponder it further because the behemoth lowers his head and steps through the hole in the wall. Powdered plaster hangs in the air, obscuring his features. He coughs, fanning away the dust. I take advantage of the moment and scramble to my feet and run out the door and into the hallway. I can hear the Candyman lumbering behind me. Though he's as large and sturdy as a brick wall, he's surprisingly fast and nimble. I'm just about to reach the living room when I feel his large sausage-sized fingers wrap around my neck and jerk me to halt. My legs fly out from under me against his strength, and I soon find myself hanging in mid-air with his hands fully engulfing my throat.

Slowly, he turns me around to face him. His eyes are

burning with fury, but his grin has spread even wider than I thought possible. He's gone completely mad.

"I didn't kill your wife," I choke out, trying desperately to pry his fingers off my neck.

"I know." His grip tightens.

My heart skips. I'm uncertain I've heard him correctly.

I'm just about to ask him to repeat what he said when the front door opens and Inspector Decroux rushes inside with his gun pointed at us.

"Monsieur Lagrange!" he shouts. "Cease this at once! Put him down now, *s'il vous plait*."

The monstrous man turns his glaring eyes from me to the Inspector. I feel his grip tightening even harder for the briefest moment. My feet dangle inches from the floor as I continue to try to pry his hands from around my neck.

"I heard a gunshot," the Candyman says. "I go to check on dear Clarise. Find d'is cretin standin' over her body, as bold as you please. Gun in hand." He growls with rage. "It's da second time he's murdered someone in my own home."

"That's a lie—erk!" He squeezes my throat tighter, cutting off my words.

"I said, release him," Decroux says again. The Inspector's gun now seems focused only on the Candyman.

"He must pay for his crimes!"

"He will. This, I promise you."

"Like he did after killin' my wife?" Jacques's hand is strangling all the air from my lungs. My world is fading in and out, as blackness edges around the periphery of my vision. "You let him escape last night!"

"It won't happen again." The Inspector steps forward. "I will watch him personally. Night and day. Until he is transported to Martinique to stand trial."

I still can't believe this is happening. The big man has just killed Clarise in front of me. In cold blood, no less. She was defenseless. Powerless to protect herself. And I'm going to be blamed for it. I just don't understand. I could understand the Candyman's hatred of me while thinking I murdered his wife, but this? This is beyond revenge. This is something else entirely.

After a moment, I feel his grip on my throat loosen, and I'm dropped to the floor in a fit of hacking coughs. Decroux moves over to me, keeping his weapon trained on Jacques as he does. He then lowers a set of handcuffs down to me. "You know how these work, no?"

I nod between coughs and work at securing my wrists with the irons. Once they're on, he steps back and looks up at the Candyman. "Now that he's secure, why don't you show me his latest victim?"

CHAPTER 19

I wait in Lagrange's living room for hours as Decroux, Chief Armad, and his two subordinates go over Clarise's murder scene with a fine-tooth comb. The Candyman's been escorted off premises while the police do their job, so I have no chance to talk with him to find out his possible motives for killing the poor girl.

After two hours pass, Inspector Decroux reappears. His face is grim as he looks down at me.

"I just don't understand, Monsieur," he says, crouching down to look me in the eye. "I've been investigating you. Talking to your known associates, as well as your friends and commanding officers in ze United States Navy. They all say you are a man above reproach. Sure, you dabble here and there with some light smuggling and bootlegging, but you've never been prone to violence. Never been in trouble with ze law, except for ze occasional bar brawl."

"I'm not hearing a question." My voice is raw from being throttled by the Candyman, but I hope my disgust carries through with my words. I'm being railroaded. As Trixie said, anyone with half a brain can see it. I'd thought that I might

145

have a chance with an unbiased outsider like Decroux, but he seems to be buying the lies—hook, line, and sinker.

"Well, I just don't quite understand," he says, standing to his full height again and looking down at me. "Why? What drives someone like you to murder not one, but two people? In ze same house? Days apart from each other?"

I chuckle. I know it sounds strange that I would laugh at a time like this, but I suppose I'm just too tired of being fearful. Too tired of running. Too tired of the whole mess. So, I shake my head and laugh.

"What is so amusing, Monsieur?"

"You are, Frenchie. You are."

His mouth gapes in surprise at my statement like he's genuinely shocked.

"How so?"

"Because it hasn't once occurred to you that you're asking the wrong questions."

One of his eyebrows raises. He begins to pace the living room floor while inserting a cigarette into a holder and lighting it up. After a few puffs, he shakes his head. "No, I'm sorry. I don't quite understand."

I stand up now. Concerned, he draws his gun on me, but I raise my shackled hands to show I'm not planning anything stupid. "The question isn't 'How could I?' The question you should be asking is 'Did I?'"

"But, of course, you did." He gestures wildly with his cigarette, reminding me a little of what Agatha Christie's Poirot might look like if he was a real person. That is, if Poirot was French, instead of Belgian. And if he was tall, skinny, and blond-haired, and wore a pencil mustache instead of his waxed one. And, of course, if he was an idiot. "Ballistics matched ze bullets of your own weapon. You were ze only one present at ze crime scene…"

"I was unconscious. And I wasn't alone."

"Oh, ze fabled American spy I've been hearing about during my investigation." His nose turns up derisively as the words leave his lips. "Your pretty little Miss Faye told me all about him. She admitted she hadn't seen him personally, though. Just heard rumors about him. And while it's true ze local constabulary has been searching for an American agent on ze island, no one I can find can admit to seeing him here ze other night."

I thumb down the hallway. "Clarise saw him."

"I interviewed her personally, Monsieur. She told me no such thing. Said you were ze only one in ze parlor that night."

I roll my eye, frustrated. We're going in circles. "She was lying. As a matter of fact, she was going to come to you later today and tell you the truth."

"So why did you kill her?"

I raise my hands in the air and scream. It's a primal scream, filled with rage and sorrow and angst. It feels great to release it all, but it draws the attention of Armad and his men, who rush into the living room from Clarise's room with their guns drawn in my direction.

"Sorry, fellas," I say, lowering my hands, and looking at the Inspector. "Look, I didn't kill her, either. Jacques did."

"And why on Earth would he do that?" Decroux asks, biting down on the tip of his cigarette holder.

"I have no idea. It didn't make any sense to me when he did it. It still doesn't. But it's the truth, and I'll swear on a stack of Bibles, too."

It's the inspector's turn to chuckle now. "Be careful, *mon ami*. You're already in enough hot water as it is. You don't want to add God's wrath to ze mix as well, do you?"

There really is no arguing with the dope. He's already made up his mind. Ballistics and flawed logic have already hammered the nail in my coffin, as far as the Inspector's concerned. The only way I can figure getting out of this mess is by solving the murder myself, but I can't do that chained in handcuffs or behind bars, and I don't see myself escaping from the Port Lucine jail a second time.

My shoulders sag in defeat. I'm at the end of my rope now, and I have no idea what I'm going to do to pull myself out.

"Look," I say, sighing. "Can you just take me to my cell now? I'm tired. I need to get some sleep, and I want to call a lawyer first thing in the morning."

Inspector Decroux nods. He's got a smug, closed-lipped grin on his face as he turns to Armad. "I'll escort ze prisoner back to ze jail and will stand guard. You three continue going over the scene for evidence, then send ze body ahead to ze pathologist in Martinique. *Comprenez vous?*"

Armad snaps his heels together and salutes. "*Oui*, Inspector. We will not let you down."

Decroux takes hold of my arm and leads me out the door. It feels a bit like what the French call *déjà vu*, as we step out into the early morning sunlight with a crowd of angry, bewildered onlookers shouting and cursing my name. This time, I see no sign of Trixie or Nessie among the throng, silently offering their love and support to my dilemma. No sign of the Candyman, either, for that matter.

I'm thankful for that small blessing. I have no idea what possessed Jacques to kill his maid and mistress. Was it because she was going to exonerate me of his wife's murder? Wouldn't that make him happy? To find out his old friend didn't kill his wife…that I hadn't betrayed him…should be cause for celebration, shouldn't it?

Wait. What did he say when I told him I didn't kill Angelique?

I don't have time to ponder my line of thought any further, however, because as Decroux leads me through the crowd, into the street, a large black sedan roars up to the curb. The crowd scatters for dear life, but the Inspector isn't quite fast enough. The chrome bumper plows into his leg, and I hear a sharp pop and a scream from the copper's lips. I whirl, watching the poor man as he falls to the ground. The bone of his femur is now sticking out through his blood-soaked pant leg, as he howls in pain. I'm just about to crouch down and help him when a pair of powerful hands grab hold of me by the arms and shoulders. I feel something hard crash against the base of my skull, and I feel myself being lifted off my feet and stuffed into the back seat of the car. The whole world flashes in a series of brilliant colors. I try to raise my head to see what's going on, but it feels like it's a thousand pounds heavier. I blink, but the haze is rapidly encroaching on my peripheral vision. I open my mouth to protest, but nothing's coming out. Then, everything goes black, and I'm dead to the world.

CHAPTER 20

As consciousness begins to drift slowly back into my world, I'm aware of a handful of things. First of all, I'm hanging in mid-air with ropes tied around my wrists and ankles. My arms feel as though they're being pulled from their sockets, and it's hard to breathe. The air is stagnant and sweltering. My clothes are wet, clinging to my skin with sweat and grime. I try to move, but I'm tapped out of any strength I hope to have.

There's also a chorus of drums beating all around me. Their rhythmic cadence vibrating down my spine with each thrust of a palm. I open my eye and see a thick roof of lush vegetation above me. Birds of vibrant colors flit from limb to limb of the trees around me, crying out their raucous songs, seemingly synchronized to the drums. I'm suspended about a foot off the ground. My feet dangle uselessly.

I turn my head and look around. Four men, bare-chested and wearing white loin cloths, sit Indian style to my right. Their hands move faster than the eye can follow, pounding down on the rawhide covers of the drums. A woman, dressed in a flowing white dress and headscarf, dances around me, her head and arms shaking convulsively with each staccato beat. A snake—it looks like a python, although they're not indigenous to the island—wraps itself around her neck, coiling itself with every move she makes.

I'm in a clearing in the middle of the jungle. I'm not sure if it's the same one I found the day before yesterday, with the Palo *nganga*, or not. But it doesn't matter. All along the clearing, their heads swaying left and right, are nearly two dozen stone-faced people, all dressed in white and glaring at me. They make a nearly perfect circle around the perimeter. King and Kong stand among them, shirtless, with their muscular arms crossed over their chests. Something tells me it's one of them that clubbed me over the head and shoved me in the back of the sedan. But if they feel smug about it, their stone-hard faces aren't showing it.

The last person is see as I scan the crowd is the immense form of the Candyman. He's in his crisp white linen suit and straw wide-brimmed hat. His face is painted again, with the all too familiar death's head of a skull. He smiles at me, revealing yellow-stained teeth, then he steps over to me. Though I'm suspended in mid-air, he still has to look down in order to meet me in the eye.

"What's going on, Jacques?"

He laughs. "You are to be a sacrifice to da gods, *Captain Joe*."

The way he says my name oozes with venom.

I also notice he used the word 'gods', not 'loa.' The loa are the spirit beings voodoo practitioners serve. They do have a god, but it's the loa they offer their sacrifices to—and never a human one. This isn't making any sense.

"The loa don't like human sacrifices, Jacques. They won't appreciate this at all."

I'm hoping my knowledge of their religion will help sway

him. No one who practices voodoo would want to make the loa angry. Human sacrifice will do just that.

Like the great showman, P.T. Barnum, the Candyman spins around for his followers, his arms outstretched. "D'is sacrifice is not to da loa!" he bellows for his congregation to hear. "D'is one is for da *older* gods. Da ones our ancestors left behind in da dark continent. Da Congo and da like."

The drum beat grows in tempo. The swaying heads and the dancing girl move frantically to keep up. Then he turns back to me and moves within inches of my face.

"But, why? Why all of this?" It's the only thing I can think of to say.

He reaches into the inside of his jacket and withdraws a long curved dagger, then leans over and whispers in my ear.

"I've wanted to do d'is for so long," he says. His breath smells of dead, uncooked fish. "You have no idea how much I despised pretending to be your friend."

My throat swells up at the words, making it hard to breathe. In all my time here, he's been like a brother to me. My best friend. And now he's telling me it's all been an act?

Then, Angelique pops into my head. Her flirtations with me. Her innuendo. Her desire to have me as a plaything. And also the words uttered just after Jacques killed Clarise. *I didn't kill your wife,* I had told him. His response was a simple two words: *I know.*

My blood runs cold.

"You killed her, didn't you?" I don't need him to respond. I already know the answer. And I already know why. I guess I've known for quite a while, although I never wanted to admit it.

"Da witch had it comin', for a long time now." He places the dagger to my throat, a silent warning to keep my voice down as we talk. He doesn't want his followers listening in on the conversation. "Always bossin' me around. Always t'inking she was in charge. Running da whole operation like da woman d'at she was. Meek. Timid. Never taking risks. I could have made us huge, if she only let me."

I try to swallow, but my throat just feels so constricted with grief.

"But Angelique found a way to hit the big time without you, didn't she?" I whisper. "She learned about classified information coming to the island. Information she could sell to the highest bidder. Information that could put her on the international playing field. Problem was, she wasn't planning on sharing it with you, was she?"

His brows furrow as he looks down at me. His malicious grin is gone, and nothing but hate burns in his eyes.

"In truth, she wanted *you* by her side." His words are little more than the hiss of a snake. With the sound of the drums beating in the air, I'm forced to read his lips to get the meaning of what he says more than actually hearing him. "It was always about you."

"Jacques, you know nothing ever happened between us. I only have eyes for Trixie, and you know it."

The dancing woman passes by my field of vision again. Her movements are now frenzied. Chaotic. From what I understand, she appears to now be in the trance-like state that practitioners call 'being ridden' by the loa. In other words, possessed by their voodoo spirits.

"Oh, Trixie." His grin is back, and it's even more maniacal than before. "Your precious songbird. If you only knew what I know about d'at girl." He pauses, his head cocking to one side. "Maybe I'll share wit' you before you die. It'll break your little white heart."

I shrug off his words. He's trying to mess with me. Trying

to play with my emotions. A cat toying with the mouse before he devours it.

"You're not listening. I would never have betrayed you, and you know it." My volume is rising, and it's rewarded by a jab to the neck. "You know it." I'm back to a whisper. "Angelique knew it, too. That's why she had Clarise drug me. She knew I would never agree to selling out my country for a price. Knew I'd never agree to cross Morris."

The Candyman sneers at the mention of his name. "Ah, yes. Your good friend Morris." He moves the dagger from my throat and begins using the blade to slice through the buttons of my shirt to expose my chest. The maniac really is planning on sacrificing me. "She drugged him, too, ya know."

I nod. "Clarise said as much."

"Want to know what happened to him?"

I blink, unsure where the big man is going with this question.

"Want to know why he wasn't d'ere, too, when you woke up?"

"Okay. Tell me."

He chuckles. "You're wrong about one t'ing, Joe. Angelique did include me in her plan for da list. At least, at first. She had no intention of keeping me after, but she needed me for da time being. She knew Morris would never give up da list's hiding spot willingly, so she drugged him. A last minute change of plans led her to drugging you as well, hoping to keep you in da dark about her little scheme."

He's now dragging the blade down my chest, slicing open a very thin sliver of skin as he does. A crimson trail starts to creep down my ribs. It stings, but at least it's not life-threatening.

Yet.

"My boys collected him from da parlor and took him to da Customs Office."

My mind flashes to the blood-coated wicker chair in the Vault.

"Monday Renot met d'em d'ere." He looks me straight in the eye. "Seems he and I managed to work out a deal, after all, regarding your cargo. Together, my boys started to work on your friend right away. Meanwhile, I stayed behind. Picked up your gun while you still slept, and put a bullet in my wife's skull, just as easy as you please."

That last part is no surprise to me. It was merely another tempt to goad me, but I'm numb to the frame job by now. I'm much more interested in what happened to Morris.

"So tell me... How did he escape?"

The Candyman's eyebrow arcs. "Escape? Who you talkin' 'bout?"

"Morris. How did he escape?"

The big man bursts out laughing, rearing back in a deep throated bellow that seems to shake the entire jungle. For a moment, the drums stop beating. The dancer comes to a halt and everyone stares slack-jawed at the outburst.

"Morris? Da only t'ing he escaped was d'is mortal coil." The drums resume their steady beat. The dancing recommences, as if never interrupted. And the Candyman leans back in, as if he's got a humdinger of a secret to tell me. "Take a look for yourself."

He gestures to my left. I turn where he's pointing, but at first I see nothing but the horde of voodoo practitioners encircling the clearing.

"No, no, no," Jacques whispers. "You gotta look up. Into da heavens."

Slowly, my eye moves up above the heads of the Candyman's followers, into the tree canopy above, and I gasp. There, nearly twenty feet in the air, hanging upside down by ropes tied around his ankles, is the bloating corpse of my old friend. Though decomposing and disfigured by the severe beating he received, he's still fairly recognizable.

There're just two things that are puzzling me. First, is the absence of his ever-present obnoxiously bright tropical shirt, which I saw him wearing the night of Angelique's murder. The second is the realization that my old friend has been dead for days. Probably since the night he was taken from the Candy-man's home and tortured. If that's the case, then who was it that shot Winston Musel on the day I escaped from jail? Whoever it was, they were wearing Morris's shirt—but it couldn't have been him.

I turn my attention back to my captor. He's showing his teeth again, proud of his handiwork. I'm appalled. I always knew the big man could be ruthless when it came to business, but I never imagined him to be so cruel. Heartless.

"You're going to pay for that."

"Maybe," he growls in my ear. "But not by you. You won't be around long enough to do anyt'ing to me."

Now, it's my time to smile. He's not expecting it from me, and it shows, with the crease in his brow.

"What? What is so amusing?"

I close my eye and take a deep, satisfying breath. I'm scared out of my mind, but at this moment, I refuse to show it.

"Killing me isn't the smartest move you've ever made," I say, a little too cocky for my own taste. But I've got to sell my bluff, any way I can.

"And why not?"

"Because, *my old friend*," I say, opening my eye and throwing him a wink. "You haven't yet found the list."

CHAPTER 21

I swear, despite the Candyman's chocolate-colored complexion, his face turns five shades of red as he glares at me. His jaw tightens. His cheeks puff out. And the point of the knife digs slowly into my neck. I feel the warmth of my own blood, as it begins to trickle from the newly punctured wound. Fortunately, he doesn't push deep, but it's enough to really get my attention.

"And I suppose you mean to tell me you know where it is?"

He's skeptical. He should be. I'm bluffing my boots off here, but with no other options, it's the only play on the table.

I try to shrug noncommittally, but hanging from my wrists as I am, I don't have the strength to pull it off. Instead, I give him a simple nod.

"Sure, I do. Morris told me where it is himself."

The drummers are still banging on their bongos like it's going out of style, but I can tell by the clumsiness of their beat that they're getting tired. I haven't seen the dancing woman pass by us in the last few minutes either. The Candyman's congregation has got to be confused as to what's going on. Sure, they're all angry with the belief that I've murdered their mamba. They want to see their high priest take his revenge on me. They just never imagined there would be this much talking during the ceremony. Then again, who likes a long-winded preacher?

"I don't believe you. Angelique. She told me you passed out, before Morris even mentioned where da list was hidden. Only t'ing that was said was d'at it was in da cargo you hauled back from Havana."

Laughing, I shake my head. "You fat-headed turnip. Morris didn't tell me where it was during Angelique's 'reading.' He told me the night before, when he approached me on my way back to the *Dream*. It was quite a surprise to see him after all these years, but after the shock wore off, he told me everything. Asked for my help. Said he didn't trust either of you two, despite having several meetings with you at your bungalow last week."

His mouth opens in surprise. He has no way of knowing that it was little Malik who told me about the frequent meetings at the Lagrange estate, but it certainly bolsters my tall tale now.

"Where is it then?" He jabs me again with the blade.

"You dumb mumbo-jumbo-spouting sack of potatoes." I'm not sure how wise it is to insult the monstrous priest, but I'm hoping to goad him into making a mistake. I just hope the mistake isn't skewering me at the point of a ceremonial knife. "Why would I tell you where the list is? It's the only thing keeping me alive."

Jacques takes a step back, scratching his chin in thought. Then, his eyes light up. I can tell you right now, I don't like the expression he's giving me one bit.

"So, you want to bargain, do you?"

"Well, the thought had crossed my mind, yeah."

He reaches into his jacket pocket, pulls out a fresh cigar, and lights it up while pondering his next move. Then, as if making up his mind, he nods and blows a thick cloud of smoke in my face.

"Okay. Here's da deal." He takes several puffs of the cigar until the tip glows with bright red embers, then takes it from his mouth and places it squarely on my stubbly cheek. The smoldering ash burns at my skin. I clench my teeth, refusing to cry out. After a moment, the cigar cools, and the pain subsides. "You tell me where da list is right now, and I don't do da same t'ing to that pretty face on Miss Trixie." He pauses, watching my reaction with feverish interest. "Only, I won't be stopping just at da face. I'll do it all over d'at luscious porcelain body of hers. And d'en, just when she can't take no more... I'll put a bullet in her head, just like I did sweet Angelique."

It's a threat I'm not expecting, and I don't have a comeback for it. He means every word. And once he's finished with Trixie, I have no doubt he'll move onto Nessie next. Then Malik. And anyone else I've ever cared about on the island.

I ponder my next words carefully. I have to. Even if I wanted to tell him, I honestly don't have a clue where the list really is. My bluff has backfired, and I've just put my closest friends in danger for nothing.

"If you touch one hair on her head, I'll..."

"What? What will you do?"

"I'll do everything in my power to force you to kill me. I'd honestly rather die than see you get what you want. It's that simple."

Then, I do the least civilized thing one man can do to another. I spit at him, hitting him right between the eyes and wiping the callous smirk from his face. I watch as his pupils dilate with rage, and he brings the dagger around to my throat once again.

"Stop!"

The voice is sharp and commanding, and it comes from somewhere behind me. The drums stop. The followers all turn their gazes in its direction. The Candyman, fortunately, also hears the command and obeys.

I hear footsteps behind me. Several. Then, three men dressed in crisp dark suits step into view. Their clothes and their hats are surprisingly clean and dry after trekking through the jungle as they have. But I guess it shouldn't be much of a surprise that KGB spies like to look their best when trying to take over the world.

I look down at them. Lamont Kingston shuffles along behind them, but his clothes haven't held up nearly as well. He's holding a machete in one hand and wiping the sweat from his brow with a handkerchief with his other. Guess Lamont gets to pull hard labor duty while he works his way up the Soviet chow line.

Alexi's here, too. The FBI man-playing-KGB agent glances up at me for the briefest of moments, before turning his attention to Jacques.

"What do you think you are doing, Comrade Lagrange?"

Comrade?

"I'm not your comrade, Krashnov. Just a businessman, looking to sell you what you're looking for," the Candyman says. He's still holding his blade awfully close to my neck.

Ah, so that explains it.

"And how do you plan to do that, if you kill the only man who knows where it is?"

The big man scoffs. "You don't really believe d'at, do you? He'll say anyt'ing to stay alive."

"The problem is, you cannot be certain that is the case.

Perhaps Morris Grant really did reveal the location of the information to him. Or perhaps he did so, and the American isn't even aware of it." He looks up at me and narrows his eyes. "Yet."

Was that some kind of message to me? A hint?

Alexi looks at Lamont and nods in my direction. "Cut him down."

The skinny porter looks from Alexi to the Candyman nervously. I watch as the voodoo man's hands begin to white-knuckle the handle of his dagger, but he relents. He steps back to allow the little spy to approach me, raise his machete, and slice through the rope that's keeping me aloft. I drop to the ground with a thud. My wrists and ankles are still bound together, but it feels like the weight of the world has been lifted from my stretched-out shoulders.

On my knees, I raise my arms up to my chest and look at Lamont. "Want to go ahead and cut these off, too, maybe?"

He sneers at me, then returns to his colleagues.

"You're an idiot, Krashnov," the Candyman says, his voice is little more than a grumbling growl. "You can't trust d'is man." He points in my direction. "He's sly, like a ferret. A born liar. He don't know where da list is, any more d'an you do."

"Captain Thacker is the one who smuggled the information from Havana," Alexi argues. "He oversaw packing the crates himself. He has got to know where the list is."

"And I'm telling you, we have searched the crate t'oroughly, Krashnov," the Candyman says. If this was a cartoon, I'd expect to see a plume of steam coming out both of his ears, as he jabs a thick finger into the spy's chest. "We've searched his boat. We've searched Nessie's bar. We've searched every possible location, and d'ere's no sign of it anywhere."

"Then how do you expect to sell the information to us? If

it's not here, then I fail to see how you can produce it. Are we wasting our time?"

"No, of course not. I'll find it. I just need…"

"And our superior has given us express orders," Alexi interrupts the big man. "The American is not to be killed, under any circumstances."

Wait. What?

Why would their boss care one way or another if I lived or died? I mean, it's true that they really have no idea how much I know or don't know. I'm their only link to Morris Grant, after all. As Alexi pointed out, I supervised the crating of the candy and booze myself. And I'm the only living person who was at Angelique's 'fortune telling' session that started it all. It would only make sense to keep me alive until they've got all their answers, I guess.

"Enough of this!" Vladimir Petrovic says. "We are taking him with us." The KGB agent I've assumed to be second-in-command steps in front of Alexi to face the Candyman. King and Kong, concerned for their priest, lunge forward, but they come to a quick stop when the third agent, Boris Usilov, and Lamont, both pull their Russian-issued guns.

Of course, you know, that's precisely when all hell breaks loose.

Enraged at the KGB men's audacity, the Candyman reaches out and grabs Vladimir by the neck. Before the others can fire off their weapons, King and Kong pounce on Boris and Lamont. The crowd of onlookers scatter, running away into the jungle. The drummers leave their drums behind and follow their fellow practitioners.

Alexi, who's been overlooked in the fracas, dashes over to me, whips out a pocket knife, and cuts the ropes from my wrists and ankles.

"Come on," he says. "We need to get…"

BAM!

A tiny red hole blossoms out from Alexi's skull, as the sound of a rifle cracks from somewhere in the jungle. He drops instantly, leaving me spattered in blood and trembling. The FBI man had only been inches away from me. Had the bullet flown just a few inches toward me, it'd be me lying dead on the damp soil right now. As for mourning the agent's passing, I have no time.

The Candyman, his goons, and the KGB boys have stopped fighting and are now looking at me, standing over the dead man.

"Ah, come on!" I shout. "You're not going to blame me for this, too, are you?"

They don't seem to be amused by my joke. Instead, they each scramble in my direction. I'm just beginning to turn around and make a break for it, when another shot echoes in the distance, and Kong tumbles forward with a gunshot wound to his chest.

"Run, Joe!" shouts a very feminine voice from the dense vegetation.

I've already guessed who my Annie Oakley rescuer is, but Trixie's voice calling out to me between gunshots cinches it. The songbird bombshell has come to my rescue all over again, and I couldn't be more grateful to her for it.

My remaining pursuers take cover behind trees, palmettos, and stones. The armed KGB agents fire wildly in Trixie's direction, and I use the chaos to make good my escape. I dash into the undergrowth, weaving my way in and out of the trees, trying to keep them as cover between me and the Reds.

Gunshots ring out, dousing the jungle in a wave of ear-splitting cracks and a cloud of smoke. Through the noise, however, I hear an enraged roar behind me. I turn to see the

Candyman's immense figure barreling through the vegetation in my direction, his dagger gripped tightly in his hand.

Like a giant, his long legs pound through the muck of the jungle floor, gaining on me with every step. I pump my legs faster, but I know it's only a matter of time before he catches up to me. My only hope is to out-distance him. Our size difference alone affords me greater endurance, and as long as I can stay a few steps away from him, he'll eventually tire himself out.

But as I've said, me and Lady Luck have never seen eye to eye. Or maybe it's just that my pursuer is better than me in every way, because in a last ditch effort to catch up to me, the voodoo gangster hurls his dagger through the air. Its blade sinks deep into the back of my shoulder, and I drop like a suitcase filled with bricks.

I'm face down in the mud, and the Candyman is on top of me before I can scramble to my feet. There's a sharp, biting pain in my back from the knife blade, which is only amplified as the big man's fists slam down into my kidneys with blinding speed. I heave for breath, but he doesn't relent. Instead, he keeps beating me from behind.

"I have had enough of you!" he screams, as he pounds my back harder, driving the little air I had out of my lungs. After a few more hits, he rolls me onto my back, driving the knife deeper. I cry out in white hot agony, which seems only to fuel his blood lust more.

His fists are now slamming into my face. I feel something pop in my nose. I think it's broken, but I'm not sure. I raise my arms up, trying to ward him off, but he bats them away as he pounds me even more.

After a moment, he seems to tire. He leans back on his knees and takes a series of deep breaths. In the momentary reprieve, I mouth the word, "Why?"

For the briefest of moments, his eyes soften.

"Because she loved you. Not me. You." He wipes the drool from his lips and his brow furrows. "It don't matter none whether you returned her love or not. You were her world. I was nothin' but hired muscle d'at she slept wit'. And I've never forgiven you for it."

Love.

It's a crazy thing.

Makes no sense half the time, and Jacques Lagrange is living proof of it.

Catching his breath, the big man shoves me onto my left side and pulls the knife from my back. He then lets me roll back and shifts his weight to straddle me.

I can hear gunshots in the distance. The KGB agents are still in a full fledged gunfight with Trixie. She might as well be a hundred miles away. She won't be able to help me this time, and it feels like the Candyman and I are the only living beings in the world.

With both hands, my old friend raises the dagger above my chest for the killing blow.

"You were like a brother to me," I manage to croak out.

"As you were to me. But I hate you with every fiber of my being for turnin' my wife's head."

I watch as the knife begins to descend, then I close my eyes tight for what I know is about to come. But a screeching howl stops death from plunging into my chest, followed by angry shouts from the Candyman himself. I open my eye to see Moe on top of the big man's back. The monkey's fingernails rake viciously at the skull-like face paint, bringing large red welts bubbling up to the surface of his skin. Before the Candyman can lash out, Moe bites down on his neck, drawing a gusher of blood.

For a moment, I'm taken aback. Vervet monkeys are

usually all bark and very little bite. They only attack when they or one of their troop are in extreme danger. So at the moment, I'm thankful that the little ball of fuzz considers me part of his family.

I'm also thankful that the monkey's attack has given me an opening. As the Candyman clutches at his now gaping wound, I wriggle out from under him and use both feet to kick him away. He falls over onto his back just as the monkey leaps to a nearby tree. But instead of running, like I should, I lunge for the big man, giving him every blow…every pounding…he's just given me. My fists slam into his face in a flurry of rage, pain, and sorrow. He squirms underneath me, trying to regain the advantage. But I don't let up.

Then, my eye catches something gleaming on the ground beside me. The knife. The Candyman must have dropped it when falling backward. Without a second thought, I reach out and grab the blade. I know I have to end this. I can't keep someone stronger than a gorilla down for too much longer. Blood loss and exertion, not to mention the conk to my head earlier and a possible broken nose, are having a heavy toll on me.

Before I can change my mind, I bring the dagger down into the Candyman's chest. He sits up from the blow, throwing me off him, as he gasps. His wide eyes look down at the blade, then over to me.

I scramble to my feet, taking a defensive stance. I've been in enough fights to know that things aren't like the way they are in the pictures. People don't just keel over and die when they get stabbed. It usually takes a while. Cause of death is usually blood loss, and for a man his size, losing enough blood to kill him will probably take a while.

"You pale piece of…" He lunges forward, knife still buried

in his chest. His hands are reaching out to me, preparing to throttle the life out of me before he bleeds out.

But just as his fingers are curling to grab my neck, there's another clap of thunder. A geyser of blood spews from a new wound in his shoulder, spinning him around. And another boom. This time, the bullet punches its way through his chest —almost dead center. He continues spinning with the momentum he's already built, then hurls to the ground and doesn't move again.

CHAPTER 22

St. Noel Island
The Next Day

I lean back in the reclining chair on the upper deck of *The Ulysses Dream*. I'm currently sipping on my third glass of rum, while enjoying the bright sun shining down on me from a clear blue sky. I'm shirtless. Trixie has just finished putting another bandage on my busted nose, and is now busy wrapping fresh strips of gauze around the knife wound in my back. Moe and Malik are playing on the dock.

It's a perfect morning in St. Noel, despite the wounds—both physical and emotional—we've all gone through for the last few days.

Inspector Decroux has just left us, heading back to the police station to write his final report on the events perpetrated by the Candyman and the rest of the motley crew searching for the classified lists. Seems I'm now cleared of all suspicions. More than a few of the Candyman's congregation had overheard enough of our conversation, when I was strung up as a sacrifice, to put the pieces together. I'm no longer on the lam, and it feels great.

"Hold still," Trixie says, pulling the bandage tighter across my chest. "You're like a child."

"Well, stop pinching me, and I will."

I reach for my jacket lying on the deck next to me and search its pockets for a fresh cigar. After a few moments, I curse.

"Joe!" Trixie glances down at the boy, then back at me.

"What are you worried about? The kid's the one that taught *me* that word." I toss the jacket back to the deck. "I'm out of smokes."

"Good. You need to give those horrible things up, anyway."

I grin at her. "I'll give them up when you agree to make an honest man out of me."

She rolls her eyes at that, then pulls the bandages even tighter, eliciting a howl from me. Then, she stands up, looks down at her handiwork, and smiles. "I should have been a nurse."

"You would have been aces at it, I can tell you that."

She takes the deck chair next to me and stares up into the sky. We sit without speaking. I'm not sure for how long, but it's a nice change of pace. After a while, like most women, she has to go and ruin the moment.

"So, do you think anyone will ever find it?" she asks, glancing at me over the rim of huge dark sunglasses.

"Find what?" I pour myself another glass from the nearly empty bottle of rum sitting on the table between us.

"You know what I'm talking about."

"The list?"

She nods.

"Frankly, I could care less."

"*Couldn't.* Couldn't care less," she corrects me, then she shifts positions in the chair and rests her body with her right elbow. "And come on. I know you care. Those secrets would do your government a lot of good." Her English is so perfect, I often forget the U.S. is just her adopted home. She's still a Hungarian citizen.

I shrug. "I'm not even convinced it was ever on the island. You know, cloak and dagger stuff. Slight of hand. Make the bad guys think it's heading to St. Noel, when it's really going to Miami instead. It's what all those spooks love doing, right?"

She pours herself a glass, finishing off the bottle, and taking a sip. "True, but what if?" She swings her legs around, sits on the edge of the deck chair, and leans toward me conspiratorially. "Those KGB guys are still out there, you know."

I cringe at the mention of those mooks. Or rather, I silently mourn the FBI agent pretending to be Alexi Krashnov. I still haven't told Trixie about him. She thought he was about to kill me when he cut my bindings. She reacted. Fired. And it was over. If she discovered he wasn't really a bad guy, I'm just not sure what that would do to her. So, I'm keeping it quiet for now. Besides, I'm still not convinced the guy's story was jake.

"They'll be caught soon enough," I tell her. "Governor Lagrange has Decroux and an entire task force from Martinique combing the island for them right now. Take it from someone who knows. This island is too small to hide out for long."

Her lips pinch together. A sure-fire sign that she's disappointed. Or miffed. I can understand why. Girl's been sheltered most of her life, until she came out to the Caribbean to make it on her own. Her head's full of those old pulp stories of spies and political intrigue. To her, finding this fabled list would be something akin to those.

Personally, I think we've had enough adventure to last a lifetime.

Trixie gets up and gathers up her medical kit and other things. "Well, Cap'n, I need to get ready for my show."

I scramble out of my own chair, careful not to reopen my wound. My back is stiff, but I'll survive. "Ah, come on, Trix. Don't be sore with me."

She smiles, then kisses my cheek. "I'm not sore, darling. We'll continue this conversation tonight. But I have a lunch-time show at Nessie's, and I'm already way past late."

I watch as she seems to glide down the gangplank to the pier, her hips swinging back and forth with each divine step. When she gets to the dock, she stops, turns to me, and blows me a kiss before making her way back up to Port Lucine.

I sigh when she slips out of sight, then I return to my chair. I grab my jacket again and do another search of its pockets, hoping a fresh batch of cigars might have just magically appeared since the last time I looked.

But me and Lady Luck. We're never going to get along.

I'm leaning back in the chair again, when Malik's voice carries up to the top deck from the pier.

"One, two, three..." The boy is playing hide-and-go-seek with Moe. Never a wise move to play that game with an alcoholic monkey, but Malik doesn't seem to mind. "...five... six...seven..."

"Malik!" I shout.

There's a pause. Then the kid lets out a curse that makes even me blush.

"Language, kid!"

"You made me lose count!" he shouts back at me.

"Yeah, but if Nessie hears you using that kind of language, you'll have to eat so much soap, you'll be crapping bubbles for weeks."

Malik giggles. A few seconds later, his head pops up on the gangplank. "Yes, Cap'n Joe? What do you need?"

I smile. Once again, the prim and proper boy we all know and love.

"I'm out of smokes," I say. "Don't suppose you have any more in that knapsack of yours, do you?"

He shakes his head. His face is dead serious now. "I'm afraid not." He moves up onto the boat, digging his hands in his pockets for something. "But maybe d'ese will help 'til I can get back from da apothecary with more."

He holds his hands out to me and drops a handful of hard candies into my palms. I nod my thanks while placing the candy on the table, and hand him some money. "Be a pal and go pick some up for me, will you?"

"Aye, aye!" Malik jerks to attention, snapping a crisp salute at me, before taking the money and running off toward town. I chuckle to myself as he speeds away. They just don't make them like Malik anymore.

Absently, I grab one of the candies, unwrap it, and pop it in my mouth. It's orange flavored and tangy, and I savor the morsel as something I might never have tasted again, if the Candyman had had his way with me. That's when I remember the monkey.

"Moe?" I shout. There's no immediate response. "Moe, the kid's gone. The game's over. You can come out now."

The monkey appears out of nowhere, clambering up the *Dream's* mooring lines and leaping into the chair that Trixie only recently occupied. He sits cross-legged, looking at me expectantly, then looking down at the candies on the table.

"I swear, monkey, your teeth are going to fall out."

In response, he just thumps his chest with a limp-wristed swat and squawks at me.

"Fine. Fine." I reach over, unwrap a piece of candy, and toss it to him. He catches it easily in his mouth.

I sit back in my chair and resume my relaxation with a deep breath. Despite the peaceful morning, the events of the past few days are whirling through my mind. The murders. The frame-ups. The spies and secrets lists. I'm still struggling to make sense of it all.

I didn't want to admit it to Trix, but the list *is* still on my mind. So are the KGB agents. Or more specifically, their head honcho. I've pretty much identified all the players on the field, but the identity of the island's top KGB stooge is still a mystery to me. And that's just troubling. Long after Vlad, Boris, and Lamont are caught, the secret agent will still be lurking somewhere on St. Noel. I can't have that.

With the political winds changing in the Caribbean, the influence of just one subversive agent could be a major game-changer for the entire world.

The list itself documents numerous Caribbean residents sympathetic to the communist cause. Each one of those names on the list has the potential of devastating the political climate of the entire world. No, I played it casually with Trixie—for my own reasons—but the truth is, I'm worried. I know I've got to find that list before anyone else does. Got to get it to Uncle Sam as soon as possible.

But the Candyman was right. They've searched the crates top to bottom, and no one found it. I know Morris was always good at the intelligence game, but wherever he chose to hide it must have been brilliant.

I reach over for another piece of candy, but all that's left now are wrappers littering the table and the deck around Moe's chair. I sit up, but the monkey's nowhere in sight.

"You little thief!" I shout. "Maybe I wanted some, too. Ever think of that?"

I chuckle while grabbing one of the candy wrappers and leaning back in my chair. Absently, my fingers glide over the cellophane wrapper, as I continue pondering everything. Besides the mysteries of the list and the KGB agent stationed permanently on the island, there's also the issue of the shooter dressed in Morris's flamboyant shirt, who shot Winston Musel. Winston himself is recovering rather nicely, according to Inspector Decroux, but someone went to a lot of trouble to make me think my old friend was still alive and looking out for me.

This whole thing makes no sense.

I turn the wrapper over in my hands, reading the little Brach's logo as I do, then I sit up instantly. Everything just clicked. The pieces of the puzzle—every last one—have fallen into place. The list. The KGB boss. Winston's shooter in Morris's shirt. All of it.

I scramble to my feet and run down into the boat's cabin before rummaging through my desk drawer for some paper and a pen. I then scribble out a hasty note, explaining everything I need, and seal it up in an envelope. Satisfied all is in order, I jog back up onto deck and begin to pace, while mentally finalizing my plans.

CHAPTER 23

I t's another twenty minutes or so before Malik returns with my cigars in hand. His face is flushed from running so fast, and I pour him a tall glass of lemonade, then mull everything over as I enjoy one of the stogies, while he catches his breath. When he's rested, I hand him the envelope.

"All right, buddy," I say to him. "I've got another job for you."

He beams at me, excited to help me however he can.

"Get this letter to Inspector Decroux. Make sure he reads it completely, got it?" He nods his understanding. "But don't tell a soul about this. I think I know where the list is."

"Whoa! Really?"

"Yep. But here's the problem. The more people who know, the easier it will be for the Reds to find out, got it? So this is probably the most important mission I've ever sent you on." I pat him on the head. "So remember, mum's the word."

"You got it, Cap'n!"

The boy takes off before I can say another thing, running down the pier and to the lane leading to Port Lucine. I smile as he goes. He's really a great kid. So eager to please. But a bit of a blabbermouth. And I know he'll have told at least ten people about the message before he ever reaches Decroux.

Then again, that's what I'm hoping for. It's the only way I can think of to draw out the KGB agents and their boss.

With my plan in motion, I slip my old .45 in my shoulder holster, pull on my flight jacket and cap, and escort Moe down into the cabin, where he'll be safe. I make sure the liquor cabinet is locked up tight, though. I really don't trust the monkey. Then, I start strolling toward the bend leading to the Customs Office. It takes me nearly twenty minutes by foot to get there, but it allows me time to cement my theories, so my plan will go off without a hitch.

When I get to the office, I find the gate locked and the dogs curled up, sleeping through the muggy morning heat. As I approach, one of them lifts a head and lets out a low growl of warning.

"Easy there, Lassie," I say to him. "You don't need to come home. I'm waiting on an invitation this time."

The dog lowers its head, and I lean against the gate post and wait. A few minutes later, I hear a motor car rumbling down the road toward me, and I know my wait—not to mention this whole mess—is almost over.

Soon, Governor Lagrange's 1936 Studebaker rolls up and crunches to a halt in front of the gate. A moment later, Inspector Decroux climbs out of the back seat. His left leg is cocooned in a plaster cast from being struck by the Candyman's car, and he's forced to walk with the help of a cane. The backseat door on the other side of the car opens and Trixie's bright smiling face appears. She rushes over to me, nearly jumping up and down with excitement.

"Malik told me you found it," she says, throwing her arms around me, while showering my face with kisses. "I knew you could do it. I just knew it!"

I take her hand in mine and give it a soft squeeze. I wish she hadn't come, but there's nothing to be done about it now. "I couldn't have done it without you, Doll."

Decroux clears his throat, interrupting our private little moment.

"As requested, I've got Chief Armad and his men escorting Monday Renot down here, as we speak," he says. "While we wait, care to fill me in on what you've discovered?"

I light another cigar and shake my head. "Not quite yet. I want the whole party to be here when I make the big reveal."

The Inspector isn't overly pleased with that, but he agrees to do things my way for the moment. After a while, the police escort stalks down the dusty road from town, with Monday bound in handcuffs for his role in the death of Morris Grant. He glares at me as they approach.

"Don't give me that look," I say to him. "You're the one who got in bed with the devil. I didn't make you do it."

He sneers in response and steps up to the gate, as Officer Marvin Conard unlocks and slides it open. Monday steps inside first, drawing the attention of the guard dogs. With a nod of his head, he sends the obedient mongrels away to disappear somewhere behind the building.

The dogs taken care of, we all make our way inside the Customs Office and to the secure door leading into the Vault.

"This is ridiculous," Monday protests. "We've already been through these crates, high and low. There's nothing here."

Marvin proceeds to unlock the padlock, and he swings open the Vault's door. The place hasn't been touched since I was here last. The bloody chair. The crimson-stained walls. The splintered crates, broken glass, and foil-wrapped candy scattered everywhere. It's all here. I suppose I can thank myself for that little blessing. Everyone was so busy trying to track me down, cleaning up the Vault was the last thing on anyone's mind.

"Oh, ye of little faith," I say to the customs agent, as I walk into the tiny room and crouch down near the remains of the crate. Trixie, practically bursting with energy, scurries over to me and kneels beside me.

"So what are we looking for, Joe?" she asks eagerly.

Ignoring her, I start sorting the discarded candies, separating the pieces by brand, shape, and size. With everyone looking on, Trixie starts helping me and cuts the time I need in two. Within ten minutes, all the candy is sorted exactly as I'd planned, and now it's time to see if my theory is actually correct.

I examine each pile, studying the wrapping, the logos, the colors—anything to help me decide the most likely answer to Morris's riddle. I think back to our conversation in Angelique's parlor. My old friend's words to me.

His last words to me, in fact.

I couldn't just fold it up and put it where it could easily be found, he'd told me. *I got pretty creative in how I handled it. Used some stuff we learned in the war...*

It's the mention of the war that triggers the answer for me. Back in the day, Morris and I rarely ever got to see each other. I was usually either flying a mission, or he was off galivanting behind enemy lines, seducing dames for information or whatever it is intelligence officers did back then. But, we developed a nifty system for messaging one another during those times where Morris had to stay incognito for a long period.

Written notes would be left, scribbled on liquor bottle labels. My favorite whiskey. Morris's favorite Chardonnay. It was a great system for just keeping up with each other as the war droned on.

Granted, the bottles inside the crate have all been smashed

to pieces. Their labels trampled underfoot and covered by cracked, drying blood. But that's not where I believe Morris would have hidden the list. He also said he'd gotten 'pretty creative.'

"Well?" Decroux asks.

Monday, Chief Armad, and his officers all squeeze through the doorway, hoping for a better view of my big reveal. Problem is, I've got to stall a bit. I want everyone at this party, after all. Not just the coppers, Monday, and Trixie.

I make a big show of examining the glass shards, picking a few pieces up. Sniffing them. Setting them back down. I crawl over to the wooden crate splinters and do the same. When I feel like I've waited long enough, my hand takes hold of one of the candies on the floor. I hold it up.

"Anyone in the mood for a sweet?" I ask.

"Joe, stop teasing," Trixie says. "Just tell us what you figured out, for crying out loud."

Smiling, I hold out the candy to her. "Seriously. Want a piece of candy?"

She rolls her eyes, then nods while holding out her hand. I unwrap the foil from the candy and hand it to her and wait for her to pop it in her mouth.

"Monsieur Thacker, I really must insist you stop wasting our time," Inspector Decroux says. "Do you know where this list is or not?"

I stand up, holding the candy wrapper out to the Inspector. "I think you'll find this interesting." Before he can take it, I take a look at the back of the wrapper. "You might want to let your government know they need to be on the lookout for some guy from Cuba named Fidel Castro," I say. "He's apparently one of the names on the list."

It's as if the Vault's jaw drops instantaneously. Everyone is staring at me like I've just grown two antlers on my head.

"It was the wrappers," I explain. "I got the candy I gave the kids a few days ago from the same wholesaler these came from. But the ones I bought personally had cellophane wrappers with company logos on them. These were just plain foil wrappers. Knowing Morris the way I did, I figured this would be the most likely place he'd hide his list in plain sight."

"It's so...so simple," Trixie says, taking the wrapper from my hand and studying the handwritten script with admiration.

It's precisely at that time that the guests I'd been expecting choose to make their presence known. KGB agents Vladimir Petrovic and Boris Usilov, along with a nervous Lamont Kingston, push through the entrance of the Vault, guns leveled at each of us.

"Thank you, Mr. Thacker," Vlad says, pointing his gun at my gut. "Obviously, we couldn't have found this without your help. Now, we'll gladly take all this candy off your hands."

I look casually from the gun to Vlad's smug face, then back at the gun, as if I have all the time in the world. Then, I hold up my index finger.

"First, it's *Captain*, not Mister." I glance over at Trixie, who's glaring the intruders down like a lioness protecting her cubs. Or, as I deduced earlier in the day, like a KGB boss playing the part of a lifetime. "Second..." I draw the gun from my shoulder holster, step over to Trixie, and wrap my arm around her—putting her between me and the gunmen. I then press the barrel of my .45 to her temple. "...you're not about to shoot me while I've got your *numero uno* dead to rights."

"Joe, what are you doing?" Trixie shouts, squirming to break free of my grip.

"*Mon Dieu!*" the Inspector cries out.

I feel Trixie's body tremble against mine, and for a moment, I hesitate with doubt. Ever since figuring out that she's the

KGB's Big Kahuna here on St. Noel, my heart has been breaking bit by bit. But I've had to maintain a brave face. I've had to go on like everything was normal. But I know the truth. I know what she is now. What she's done. And as much as she means to me, I can't let her get away with it.

The KGB men look at each other, confused. They're not sure how they're supposed to react. What they're supposed to do. It's the last thing they've prepared for, which is precisely why I've chosen it for my end game.

"Sorry, Trix," I say into her ear. The involuntary whiff of her perfume nearly makes me falter for a second time in as many minutes. I tell myself I've got to be strong. "But the jig, as they say, is up. I know you're the KGB top dog here, though for the life of me, I can't figure out why. With what the Reds have done to your country…your people…how can you agree to work with them?"

She opens her mouth, as if to protest, but sighs instead. "How did you know?"

"Lots of little things, really." I keep my attention fixed on her comrades while pressing the gun against her head. "The biggest clue was your constant insistence that I go search for the list. Even after I was arrested, accused of Angelique's murder, your first instinct was to send me on a search for it, rather than to try to clear my name. You've kept after me to find it ever since. That alone was kind of suspicious, but understandable for an adventurous spirit like you.

"But then there's your eavesdropping. Spies are notoriously careful about where they talk business and who's around when they do. Yet, you seemed to overhear an awful lot about what was going on. You were able to keep me informed about what your comrades were up to. Of course, I didn't really think about it at the time. I had a lot on my mind, after all. But once the dust settled with the Candyman's frame job, it gave me time to really think things through."

Boris steps forward, aiming his weapon at us. "Enough of this! Do you really think threatening Miss Faye will stop us from completing our mission? No one is above Mother Russia. I'd just as soon put a bullet in her than…"

I turn my gun on him and pull the trigger. I'm aiming for his chest. The bullet splits his skull. He falls backward, into the arms of his compatriots, who both look at me with horror in their eyes.

"I'm. Not. Finished." My eye could burn a hole right through them. My heart is aching. My soul is fractured. I love this woman with all my heart, yet I sympathize with Boris's sentiment. No one is above sweet Lady Liberty. "Now, every-one. Drop your weapons unless you want to join him."

Vlad and Lamont do as I say. Their guns clatter to the floor. Chief Armad and his own little gestapo seem to think my command is directed at them as well, because they follow suit. I don't mind. Only Inspector Decroux is level-headed enough not to disarm himself in the little standoff.

So the man has more sense in his head than I first thought.

"Where was I?" I ask, letting Trixie go, but keeping my gun on her all the same.

"You were explaining how you knew about me."

"Oh yeah. That." For someone who's been caught at espi-onage and possible treason, her soft narrow face is serene. If I'm not mistaken, there might be a hint of relief in her eyes, but that might just be me seeing what I want to see. "Well, you're an excellent shot with a rifle. You proved that yesterday at the Candyman's voodoo ceremony. Not only did you end the fat man's life, but you put a bullet in Alexi's head from a hundred yards away." I look her in the eye. "You knew he was FBI, didn't you?"

She nods.

"Thought so. So, it only took a little hindsight to also tell me you were the one dressed in Morris's shirt, who shot poor Winston the night of my escape. You were too far away to have used a pistol. It had to be a rifle. Apparently, your weapon of choice. You wanted me to think Morris was still alive...to keep pushing me to get to the list, for the sake of my friend."

"I felt horrible about Winston," she says. "But I had to keep you free. To find the list."

I offer her a nodding frown. I truly believe she means it. She does feel bad about shooting the man. But I need to press on before I lose my nerve.

"Then, there was the nail in the coffin's lid. Out there in the Candyman's ceremonial circle, Alexi told him that his boss didn't want me harmed under *any* circumstances." I shake my head, hating myself for feeling the way I do. "Even as a KGB spy, you loved me. You really do love me."

Her eyes glisten. A single tear runs down her cheek, and she nods. "Yes. I do."

They're the two words I've wanted most to hear come from her lips since I've known her. 'I do.' And yet, hearing them now threatens to send me over the edge.

I take a deep breath, collecting myself. Wiping my own tear from my face and willing myself to become cold and indifferent to this woman.

"Anyway, when I figured out Morris's little hiding spot for the list, I also knew I needed to lure your comrades out of hiding. I sent that note with Malik, making him promise not to tell a single soul where I was going."

She smiles at that and laughs quietly. "Knowing full well that little monster could never keep anything secret. You knew he would tell me, didn't you?"

I nod. "I really hoped I was wrong about you. But when

you got out of the car with the Inspector here, I was crushed. But I knew you would have sent word to your goons to come. I just had to wait long enough for them to sneak into the building before I revealed everything."

"You should have been a detective." Her smile is warm and genuine. It's also very sad. "You should know. I've never worked for the Soviets under my own volition. They've imprisoned some of my family. My grandparents. Cousins. I can't say they *forced* me to work for them, but they've promised their freedom in exchange for my cooperation here. It was a bargain I just couldn't pass up."

I want to go to her. Take her in my arms one last time. But I tell myself I can't. If I do, I doubt I'll find strength enough to let her go. Instead, I turn to Inspector Decroux, and nod. At my signal, he places a whistle to his lips and blows. A few moments later, the sound of several boot heels echoes through the building. Ten heavily armed men—part of the task force from Martinique that was sent here to track down the Reds— appear in the Vault's door to arrest Trixie, Vladimir, and Lamont.

I walk out of the Vault...shoulders sagging, hands in my pockets...as the officers busy themselves with handcuffing the love of my life. I won't look back. I can't. Instead, I walk out of the building and up the beach leading to the pier and my boat. And an alcoholic monkey with a candy fixation.

EPILOGUE

Port Lucine Jail
Two Days Later

oday's the day. By dawn, Trixie's fate will be sealed. From what she's heard, the sea plane is currently on its way to St. Noel to transport her and her crew to Martinique, to face trial by a French court for espionage and treason. She's even heard rumors that she might face charges by the Americans, too.

Although she lived in New York since she was barely a teenager before she moved to the islands, she never became a citizen there. She's probably not entirely sure how they could try her as a traitor there, but then again, politics never worry about fairness, or their own laws, for that matter.

But as she sits with her back against the hard stone wall, knees raised to her chest and arms hugging her knees, she no longer seems to care what happens to her. She has no love for the Soviet Union. She harbors no loyalty to the communists. Nor does she care about the French or the Americans. The only thing she's ever loved is now out of her reach. Forever.

Sure, she played it cool with me for years. Teasing me. Leading me on. Never daring to allow me to get too close. Always keeping me at arm's length. She had to. She couldn't afford to fall in love with an American ex-pilot-turned-charter-boat-captain. She failed miserably at that. She couldn't help herself. Guess I was just too charming not to flip head over heels for.

Then, I discovered her dark secret. Her clandestine occupation. And she broke my heart. She could see it in my eye in the Vault. I was devastated, no matter how hard I tried to hide it. Trixie had hurt the only man she ever truly loved, and now it looks like it's tearing her apart.

She shifts in her bunk, staring into the next cell over, where her 'comrades' now sleep peacefully. She might envy their commitment to the 'cause,' which allows them to sleep without worry, because of their own misguided delusions of patriotism.

She didn't ask for any of this. Just as I said, she despises what Russia has done to her people. Reviles the prison camps they send Hungarian upstarts to...upstarts like her elderly grandparents.

In many ways, she looks like she feels as though she should curse me. If it wasn't for me, she would have completed her mission, and her family would now walk freely through the streets of Budapest. But her feelings for me compromised her mission. Divided her focus, not to mention her loyalties.

She closes her eyes, probably hoping sleep will take her away from the turmoil rumbling in her soul. The hay that makes up her mattress is lumpy. Uneven. Digging into her back. I should know. The same lumpy unevenness did its number on my back just a few days ago.

She might even be thinking about how I hid in the cot to

effect my escape. How I escaped into the night, with *her* help. She had no idea at the time that it would be the beginning of the end for her. Sure, she wanted the list. It was her mission. But she also didn't want me to hang for a murder she knew Jacques Lagrange had committed.

She rolls over onto her side, facing the wall of her cell. She traces the cracks within the mortar with her eyes, probably letting the patterns lull her into twilight sleep. She's just about to drift off when something drops down on top of her. She rolls out of bed, throwing what fell on her to the floor. But it leaps into the air, latches onto the bars of her cell, and hangs there with a sharp-toothed smile on its face.

"Moe?" she whispers. She glances over at her men in the next cell, who don't seem to have been disturbed by the commotion.

The monkey scrambles up the bars, latches onto a cross beam with its tail, and hangs upside down. There's something shiny in its tiny hands.

"What do you have there, Moe?" she asks.

She holds out her hands, palms up, and the monkey drops a key into them. The key to the cellblock.

She blinks. It's just like what she did for my own breakout.

Excited, she leaps onto her bed and jumps up to the small window above her bunk, clinging to the bars with her hands.

I'm smiling back at her through the opening.

"The way I see it," I say, nodding at the cell doors behind her, "we found the list. It's safely being sent to the U.S., as well as the French government. We stopped the killer of a double murder. And we caught a bunch of KGB spies trying to turn the Caribbean against good ol' Uncle Sam."

She stares up at me, bewildered by it all. Unsure of what I'm getting at.

"And I'm neither a spy nor a law man," I continue. "Heck, on the high seas, I'm as free as a bird."

"Wh-what are you saying, Joe?"

My grin spreads wider, and I hold up the keys to the *Dream*. "Fancy a trip to freedom?"